SWEET PIZZA

G. R. GEMIN

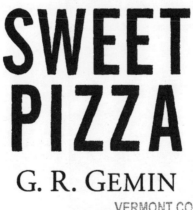

nosy
crow

Praise for
COWGIRL

Shortlisted for the UKLA Book Award
Shortlisted for the Branford Boase Award
Winner of the Tir Na n-Og Award

Cowgirl has been adapted as a play by Oxford University Press.

"Ridiculously lovely and entrancing. This is a book written with a lot of love, a lot of passion, (a lot of cows!) and I'm so glad it exists."
Daisy Johnson, *Did You Ever Stop to Think...*

"Authentic, charming and narrated by a relatable, standout voice. It cheered me right up."
Pretty Books

"Friendly, refreshing and absorbing. *Cowgirl* is a great read."
My Book Corner

"Perceptive, down-to-earth and eminently readable. I really enjoyed this."
Parents in Touch

"Funny, moving and thoughtful. I thoroughly enjoyed this impressive debut."
The Bookbag

For
Mamma, Barbara and Isabelle
For all the lovely food

First published in the UK in 2016 by Nosy Crow Ltd
The Crow's Nest, 10a Lant Street
London, SE1 1QR, UK

Nosy Crow and associated logos are trademarks and/or registered
trademarks of Nosy Crow Ltd

Text © G. R. Gemin, 2016
Cover artwork © Tom Clohosy Cole, 2016

The right of Giancarlo Gemin to be identified as the author of this work
has been asserted by him in accordance with the Copyright, Designs
and Patents Act, 1988

1 3 5 7 9 10 8 6 4 2

A CIP catalogue record for this book is available from the British Library

Printed and bound in the UK by Clays Ltd, St Ives Plc
Typeset by Tiger Media

Papers used by Nosy Crow are made from wood grown in
sustainable forests.

ISBN: 978 0 85763 630 0

www.nosycrow.com

ONE

Joe loved fried chicken and chips smothered in tomato sauce and mayonnaise, especially after a day at school – nothing else hit the mark as far as he was concerned.

As he walked home with Combi he was feeling glum, and the grey sky and rain didn't help his mood. When they reached Bryn Mawr High Street he knew Combi was heading for the Chicken Box, and he could see lots of children outside the shop.

"Don't want any," he said.

"Any what?" asked Combi.

"Chicken and chips."

"Why?"

"Mam said I mustn't. No more fizzy drinks either."

"How come?" Combi asked as he stopped in front of the takeaway.

Joe gazed at the children all around him, tucking into the boxes of chicken and chips. "She reckons I'm overweight." He waited for Combi to express surprise, but Combi just stared at him. "Doesn't your mam go on at you?" Joe asked.

"'Bout what?"

"Being overweight."

Combi's lip curled. "I'm not though."

For a moment Joe thought he was joking. "You're as big as me!"

"But I'm in proportion," Combi said as he went into the shop.

In proportion to what? Joe wondered.

He had hoped Combi would show solidarity and not buy any, so he felt let down. The rain drummed on his hood as he waited. He wished he had an umbrella, however uncool. The noise of the children eating all around him seemed to get louder and louder, like hyenas munching on a wildebeest, and the smell of the chicken was so strong his mouth filled with saliva.

Combi came out with the Chicken Box Deal

and stood in front of Joe as he ate. "Oh, go on, 'ave some," he said, his mouth smeared in sauce. "I won't grass on you."

Joe glanced up the High Street towards Cafe Merelli. He looked down at the chicken and chips, fast disappearing.

He swallowed.

"We've got to finish it before we get to the cafe."

TWO

When Joe and Combi entered Cafe Merelli, Joe's mam was behind the counter gazing out of the window, her eyes fixed and staring. "'Lo, Mam," he said.

"Hello, love." She blinked and sniffed the air. "Can I smell chicken and chips?"

"It was mine," said Combi. "Joe never had any. Honest, Mrs Davis."

"Did I ask?" She glanced at Joe, who licked his lips. "You must be hungry then?"

"Yeah."

"That's good," said Mam as she took a plate from

inside a glass cabinet. "I did you a tuna salad, heavy on the cucumber."

"Ta," said Joe.

"Can I have a Coke, please, Mrs Davis?" Combi asked.

"Glass?"

"No, thanks."

As Mam turned to get a Coke out of the fridge, Joe elbowed him and frowned.

What? mouthed Combi.

Coke! Joe mouthed back, just as Mam turned and plonked the can on the counter.

"Glass of water, Joe?" asked Mam.

"Please," he said, forcing a smile.

Mam handed him the glass of water and he went to sit in a booth with Combi.

Cafe Merelli had seen better days: the Formica wall panels were dirty and cracked in places; the red faux-leather seating was worn and dotted with taped repairs; and the vinyl floor tiles were peeling – it was all suffering from long-term neglect.

A pensioner, sitting at one of the other tables, was craning her neck. "Joe. Can you see if the bus is coming?"

Joe leaned close to the window and took a peek up the road. "Not yet, Gwen."

"Oh, desperate to get home, I am," she said. "My feet have swelled to twice their size, and I don't want to be late for *Flog It*."

Joe watched Combi's Adam's apple bob up and down as he gulped the drink, and then he paused for breath. "Chicken and chips always makes me so thirsty."

"Really?" said Joe as he picked at his salad.

Then his attention was caught by Vaughan, the only other customer in the cafe – he had a perplexed expression on his face, with his mouth hanging open, and he was scratching his armpit. "Hey, Joe," he said. "Just saying to your mam ... you can't tickle yourself."

Joe glanced at Mam, who rolled her eyes.

"Someone *else* can tickle you," Vaughan said, "but *you* can't tickle yourself. Try it. Go on."

"Take your word for it," said Joe.

He noticed Combi slip his hand up to his armpit. "It's true," said Combi, then he arched back, guzzling more of his Coke.

"Look at that!" said Joe.

Combi stopped drinking, which was what Joe wanted. He pointed at a framed newspaper page. "We put the article about Nonno on the wall."

"I seen it," said Combi.

"Not on the wall, you haven't," said Joe. "We only

6

put it up this morning."

"I seen the article though – all about your granddad when he turned ninety."

"It's good, innit?" said Vaughan. "'*Beppe Merelli – the last of the original Italian cafe owners in Wales*'," he read out loud. "Proud to know him, I am."

Joe turned and smiled. He pointed at a black-and-white photograph alongside the article. "And that's my Nonno stood outside this very cafe—"

"In nineteen fifty-three," interrupted Combi. "I know, I know."

Joe went to speak, but Combi pointed at another photograph. "And that's the cafe the year it opened in nineteen twenty-nine," he said. "With your granddad's dad, Vito Merelli, stood outside. See? I know."

"You dissing my family?" asked Joe.

Combi screwed up his nose. "No."

"What's wrong with being proud of my Italian roots?"

"Because you're Welsh."

"I'm Italian!"

"Welsh."

"So you're not Afro-Caribbean then?" Joe asked.

"I'm Welsh," said Combi. "And Afro-Caribbean on my dad's side, but I don't go on about it. Not like you, '*Oh, I wish my name was Joe Merelli instead of Joe Davis*,'" he said in a whiny voice. "'*It sounds SO much better...*'"

Joe kicked him under the table.

"Did you *say* that?" Mam asked.

"I can't remember," said Joe, narrowing his eyes at Combi.

"Well, I apologise for not consulting you on the choice of family I married into, Joe," said Mam. "But you weren't born!"

"Merelli *is* a lovely name," said Gwen. "Has to be said."

Joe smiled, then he caught Mam's eye. "I see there's taekwondo classes on at the Community Centre," she said. "Shall I put your name down, Joe?"

Combi stopped drinking his Coke and glanced at him.

"Oh, Mam. What for?" said Joe.

"Get you fit."

"Not taekwondo, Mam."

"Why not?"

Joe couldn't think of a reason.

"I heard someone died of taekwondo," said Combi.

Joe pointed at him. "See!"

Mam tutted. Combi held out the can of Coke to Joe, like a peace offering. "Want some?"

Joe kicked him under the table again. "No thanks, Combi," he said aloud, sliding his eyes in the direction of Mam. "It's all sugar. Besides, it's a conflict of interest."

"Conflict of interest? How?"

"I can't sell a customer a Coke and then drink some, can I?"

"But your mam sold it me."

"Yeah, but this is my cafe, Combi."

"Oh, and it's a goldmine," said Mam, still staring out into the High Street.

"You dissing the cafe, Mam?" said Joe, but before she could reply the door behind the counter opened and there stood Joe's granddad.

"Hi, Nonno!" Joe called.

"Hello, Mr Merelli," said Gwen and Vaughan. Combi raised his can of Coke.

Nonno smiled and nodded at his faithful customers. He was tall and his voice was deep and soft. "Going for a *passeggiata*, Lucia."

"OK," said Mam.

Joe always accompanied Nonno for his evening stroll. He watched his granddad button his overcoat, neatly fold a scarf under the lapels and run his fingers round the rim of his felt hat.

"See you tomorrow, Combi," said Joe. "Or, as I'm

Italian, I should say, *a domani*! "

"What about your salad?" said Mam.

"I'll have it later," said Joe.

As he stepped outside with Nonno, Joe couldn't resist a glance back at Combi, who pointed at him and shouted, "Welsh, you are!"

Joe saw the bus turn on to the High Street.

"Gwen!" he called, banging on the cafe window. "Bus!"

He waved for the bus to stop as Gwen hurried out of her booth.

THREE

"No one does the *passeggiata* round here, do they, Nonno?" Joe said as they walked along. "'Specially in the rain."

Nonno shook his head. "Just us."

Joe had been to Italy only once, when he was eight. It was a faded memory, but he remembered Nonno explaining *la passeggiata* – people strolling in their town centre in the late afternoon, even in winter.

"It's nice to see people wandering about and chatting," said Nonno. "It's like marking the end of the day, and it makes you feel you belong."

"Yeah," said Joe, even though he wasn't exactly

sure what he meant. "The Welsh are Italians in the rain," he added. It was an old phrase he knew would make Nonno smile. The wind had picked up but it didn't deter them.

"Taking your constitutional, are you, Beppe?" asked Mr Lewis the butcher as he hurried by.

Joe liked the fact that he had the same name as his granddad. "If Beppe is Italian for Joe, how come my name's Joe and not Beppe?"

Nonno pulled down the edges of his mouth. "Your mam thought you should be Joe, as you've got a Welsh surname."

Joe felt a twinge of guilt knowing Mam had found out he preferred the surname Merelli.

After they walked a little more, Nonno stopped. "Your mam's gonna sell, Joe."

"Definitely?"

Nonno gazed across the street and gave the tiniest nod. "She called the estate agent," he said. "Maybe it's time."

"I don't get why," said Joe.

"Look." Nonno waved a hand towards the shops on the opposite side of the High Street. "It's terrible, Joe. Once there were lots of shops. Lots of business. I'm talking many years ago. The old Bracchi cafe is gone – a betting shop now... People just don't stay long when they come to the High Street any more."

Joe scanned the shops that were left – a betting shop, a butcher's, a few takeaways, including the Chicken Box, the Co-op and Post Office, and Mr Malewski's Emporium. The rest were closed down.

"Malewski's is always busy," said Joe as they stopped in front of the shop that sold products from Eastern Europe. Mr Malewski waved from inside the store and Nonno waved back. "Nice man. Good business."

"Mam says the Eastern Europeans are taking over the town," said Joe.

"They come here and they work hard," said Nonno. "Just like my Papà did."

Joe hated the idea of Cafe Merelli closing. "But I love the cafe," he said, looking up at his granddad.

Nonno smiled. It was a sad smile, it seemed to Joe, and Nonno's hand was heavy as it fell on his shoulder. His granddad's eyes were watering, but Joe couldn't be sure if it was the wind or if he was crying.

FOUR

The kitchen behind the cafe was where Joe and his family ate their meals and cooked food for the customers. There was a dining table, and shelves stocked with supplies of takeaway cups, napkins, condiments and tins of various foods.

Joe helped Nonno prepare dinner in the kitchen; it was an established routine. Tonight they were making lasagne, Joe's favourite. Nonno hummed along to one of his opera CDs while he cooked.

"Which opera's this then?" Joe asked.

"Verdi's *La Traviata*," said Nonno.

"What's 'appening?"

14

"Violetta's dying."

"Aw, right... Why they always dying?"

Nonno pulled the corners of his mouth down. "That's opera."

Joe loved helping Nonno fill the baking tray with sheets of pasta, minced meat with tomato, and the white sauce.

It wasn't long before Joe's dad came in noisily through the back door.

"All right, Joe. Beppe?" He went straight to the sink to wash his hands. "Three new double wall sockets I did for Mr Choudary," he said. "All in an hour and no redecorating needed."

"Nice one," said Joe.

Dad dried his hands and put his arm round Joe's shoulder. "Smells fabulous. Teaching him well, you are, Beppe."

Nonno smiled and nodded, just as the door to the cafe opened and Mam came in. She switched off the lights behind her and Joe saw the cafe in darkness before she closed the door. "Another action-packed day over," she said, before greeting Joe's dad with a kiss.

Joe started setting the table. "Mam, you definitely selling the cafe then?"

"Yes, Joe," she said. "That cafe is not what it was –

hasn't been for years. Not since I was a girl."

"But, Mam, I thought that when I'm sixteen I'd take over. You can retire."

"Retire? Get him. And take over what, Joe?" she asked. "What you don't realise is that what pays the bills here is not the cafe..." She nodded at Dad. "It's your father with his electrician work – he brings in money for us to live here. The only thing that makes this house different from any other is that room through there…" She pointed at the door to the café. "It opens on to the High Street and people walk in for a hot drink, a stale bun and a sit-down. That's the only difference. It's not a charity, Joe."

"Yeah, but—"

"I can't remember the last time someone ordered food, aside from breakfast," said Mam. "When I open that till of an evening, there's barely enough to cover the heating and light, let alone a wage."

"But where would we live?" Joe asked.

"We could buy a small house, by the sea in Penarth maybe. I'll get a job – don't mind what I do – Nonno can take it easy, and Len carries on doing his electrics."

Nonno opened the oven and brought the sizzling lasagne to the centre of the table.

"*Pronto*," he said.

"Don't forget your side salad, Joe," said Mam.

Everyone took a seat.

Joe watched Nonno dishing out the steaming lasagne. They started eating and chatting about their day, but Joe suddenly didn't feel hungry. He glanced at the door that led into the cafe. He was Joe Davis, heir to Cafe Merelli of Bryn Mawr. If it was sold he'd just be Joe Davis who lives in a house. It wasn't the same.

FIVE

Joe thought it was funny that he lived in Wales and yet they had relatives in Italy.

"Mimi sends her love," said Nonno, peering at the laptop screen.

Joe's lip curled up. "She got on my nerves when we went over there."

"She's your only cousin, Joe."

"Second cousin. Dragged me around and talked non-stop, and she said I ate too much ice cream. 'Gelato Joe', she called me."

Nonno chuckled, then he grew serious and shook his head. "There's no work out there, she says. She's working in a coffee bar. It's a waste – she's a very good cook. We ought to invite her over here."

"What for?" Joe said, thinking of Mimi telling him he was overweight, and Mam agreeing.

"She'd get a job far more easily here," said Nonno. "We could offer good Italian food." He slowly typed a reply on the laptop. "History repeats itself, Joe."

"How d'you mean?"

"Well, your great-grandfather, Vito, came here because there was no work in Italy, back in nineteen twenty-five. Now Italians and Romanians and Polish, and all nationalities, come over for work, see, just like my dad."

"Mam moans about the Eastern Europeans, doesn't she?" said Joe.

"She shouldn't," said Nonno. "It's natural to seek work to earn money and better yourself. They work hard too."

"Nonno, you said you were going to tell me the history of the cafe, after that newspaper man came to interview you the other week. You said you were going to record it as a ... as a something-or-other..."

"Oral history," said Nonno.

"That's it. Well, we should. I mean, you should do it."

"Sure," said Nonno as he typed.

"I'll get your old tape recorder," said Joe.

"What, now?"

"Why not?"

Nonno smiled. "OK."

Joe sensed that Nonno was a bit shy to start. So he asked him something he'd never thought about until that moment. "Nonno, what that newspaper article didn't explain was why Italians came to Wales in particular?" He pressed the record button on the tape recorder.

"The Italians were everywhere, Joe. All over South Wales," said Nonno. "They came because South Wales had enough coal to supply the world – they just needed to get it out of the ground. Most of the Italians came from northern Italy, especially from the Bardi region. They came for the work, but where there's work people need to eat. So they also came to feed people, and when they had enough money they opened cafes. That's what Papà did before I was born."

"What did he think of the Welsh?" Joe asked.

"Oh, he loved them – they're people with song in their soul. That's what makes Italians and Welsh fit together so well, I think. Papà always had music on in the cafe, a bit of Verdi or Puccini, or Neapolitan songs. He was always ready to help people too, whether they were Welsh or Italian recently arrived, or anyone for that matter. There were people from other parts of Europe back then, just like now."

"What about the cafe?" Joe asked. "I mean, when it first opened."

"Oh, the Italian cafes were popular – a place to gather, see, Joe. Somewhere to be. Cafe Merelli was always busy, right from the off. We sold tea, coffee, all sorts of provisions. Back then people didn't know about Italian food – now you find it all over the world, of course. In the summertime we sold ice cream. Papà would stand in the doorway of the cafe in his white overcoat and straw hat, look up at the sky and say, '*Beppe! Vai a vendere gelato.*' I was always a little bit nervous pushing the cart round the streets, but out I went. I was about your age, Joe. I'd ring a bell and call out '*GELATO!*', which everyone got to know was Italian for ice cream. And it wasn't long before I had a queue. I'd scoop out a ball and press it into a cone. Sometimes I'd give a bit more if it was a friend or a girl I'd taken a fancy to."

"So why were you nervous?" Joe asked.

"Oh, there were a few boys who threw their weight around. I remember one day I was selling loads of ice cream as it was hot, then Johnny Corbett showed up with a couple of his mates. 'Give us one then,' he said. I scooped a ball of ice cream, put it in a cone and gave it to him. 'Us too,' the other boys said. So I made up two more. 'Three pennies, please,' I said, holding my hand out.

"'Didn't know we had to pay for them,' says Johnny. 'Should've said that before you give 'em!'"

"What an idiot," said Joe.

"He wouldn't have done it if people were around. He said to me, 'I thought you Eyeties were giving ice cream free as we've given you work and a place to live.' I was angry knowing how hard Papà and Mamma worked. 'Pay me,' I said, though I knew I was in trouble. 'Gonna make me, are you?' he said."

"What happened?" asked Joe.

"They set about me. I gave as good as I got, mind, but they tipped the cart over and ran off. When I got back here I went in through the backyard, but Mamma could see something had happened, with the marks on my face and my jacket torn. They didn't take the money though, and that's all I really cared about.

"Mamma cleaned me up. 'Please don't tell Papà,' I said. She kissed me on the forehead and held up a finger, like a warning. 'For now I keep quiet ... for now.'

"In the cafe I felt safe, see – it was my territory. My cafe."

Nonno smiled and paused. "It's good that you want to hear the story, Joe, but I'm tired. Little at a time, yeah?"

"OK. No problem."

"Stay and listen to some opera with me, Joe."

Nonno put on *La Traviata* by Verdi again.

"Lovely music," said Joe, but for the first time he actually meant it.

SIX

The next day after school Nonno had a doctor's appointment, and Joe said he'd go with him. The doctor's waiting room was as full as a tin of tomatoes by the time they got there.

"Hello, Beppe," said Lilly Matthews as they entered.

"*Ciao*, Lilly," said Nonno. He took her hand and kissed it.

"Always the gentleman. How are you?"

"Fine. You been waiting long?" he asked her.

"Over half an hour, and there's loads that were here before me."

Nonno gazed around the waiting room and said, "You see the people here, Joe? This is how full the cafe used to be. Remember, Lilly?"

"I remember," she said. "Hub of the town, Cafe Merelli was."

Nonno smiled. "Never quiet in the cafe – there was always people. Always."

An announcement came over the tannoy. "*Lilly Matthews to Dr Dhital, room two.*"

"About time," said Lilly as she got up.

Nonno patted Joe's hand. "It's a pity that the cafe's not as full as this waiting room any more."

Joe felt sad for him, especially after the story he'd told on the tape.

Later, when they were called through, Nonno had to remove his shirt so that the doctor could listen to his chest. The sound of his long, heavy breaths filled the room. Nonno gave Joe a wink but he seemed older somehow, and more frail, and it made Joe feel uncomfortable – almost as if he was frightened of something.

Every morning Nonno opened the cafe to help cook the breakfasts. Joe helped out too, as it was the only time of day that business was brisk.

While Joe had his own breakfast in the cafe he

watched Nonno serve – he was always smartly dressed in his white coat and hat. "Help yourselves to sauce, gentlemen," he said as he put the plates down before the customers. "If you want more tea or coffee, just say. No extra." Then he was back behind the counter watching over everyone or tidying things away. Joe had once heard someone describe Nonno as dignified, and he thought it was just the right word. The cafe doorbell rang and in walked Vaughan. "Morning, Mr Merelli – usual, please."

Nonno gave him a nod. "Certainly. Straight away."

Vaughan sat down opposite Joe. "How's it going?"

"Fine."

"What you eating?"

"Tea. Scrambled eggs on toast."

"Lovely. Set you up good," said Vaughan. "Funny, isn't it? You'd never have those eggs, toast and tea all mashed together on a plate, would you? But once it's in your stomach, where it's all mixed up, it doesn't matter, does it?"

"Well, you don't have taste buds in your stomach," said Joe.

"That's right," said Vaughan. "Still weird though."

"What's on the agenda today then?" Joe asked him, thinking it was a good customer-relations question, which is something Nonno had always told him was important.

"I got an appointment at the Job Centre at eleven, but I want to get away sharp as I've loads to do on my allotment, and *Jason and the Argonauts* is on telly, half-two."

"What's that? Film?"

"Aye. Fantastic. Special effects by Ray Harryhausen – the statue of Talos coming to life is my favourite bit. I got the DVD but there's something nice about watching a film when it's on the telly – all cosy. Know what I mean?"

Combi came into the cafe, holding a half-eaten iced finger. "Joe! Coming to school?"

Joe got up reluctantly, as he wanted to stay in the cafe a little longer. Nonno brought Vaughan a cup of tea and placed a hand on Joe's shoulder. When Joe glanced up into his eyes the uneasy feeling came to him again.

"Work hard," Nonno said as he picked up the empty plate and mug.

Joe felt a shudder of fear as he watched Nonno walk back behind the counter.

SEVEN

Joe left school to have lunch at home, as usual, but today he was anxious, as if something was wrong. When he got to the cafe he saw Gwen in her usual place, and Mam was chatting to Combi's mam, Natalie.

"Hello, love," said Mam. "I did you egg salad."

"I just want to see Nonno first," said Joe. "Where is he?"

"In the back."

Joe went through, but Nonno wasn't in the kitchen. He went upstairs to the lounge. "Nonno!" he called out.

He made his way up to Nonno's room at the top of the house. He knocked on the door, but there was no answer. His heart started thumping as he entered.

Nonno was sitting in his armchair. His face was sort of twisted. He opened his mouth, but seemed to have difficulty speaking as he reached out to Joe.

"It's OK, Nonno," Joe said as he took his hand, even though he knew everything was far from good. He phoned for an ambulance. "It's my Nonno, I mean my granddad... Something's wrong. Come quickly, please!" He gave the address as he ran downstairs and into the cafe. "Mam! It's Nonno!"

Joe told her the ambulance was on its way, and they went back upstairs. When Mam saw Nonno she started to cry.

Joe felt useless as they waited for the ambulance, and then he had an idea.

It was a strange thing to do, but he picked out *La Traviata* and put it in the CD player. "What are you doing, Joe?" asked Mam.

"It's OK," he said.

They sat with Nonno, holding his hand and listening to the beautiful music until the ambulance arrived.

EIGHT

The next day the cafe was closed.

Nonno had never been ill before, other than the odd cold. Fit as a fiddle, Mam used to say, but now he'd had a stroke. They all stood at the end of the hospital bed looking down at him. He was still confused. Joe held his breath in intervals to try and stop himself crying, but it didn't help.

As soon as they got back to the cafe Joe went upstairs to write to Mimi on the laptop, as he thought she'd like to know what had happened. He explained that Nonno was unable to use one of his arms, or walk unaided. The doctor had explained that physiotherapists would help him recuperate, but that it would take many months.

After he sent the message Joe wandered up to Nonno's bedroom and noticed the tape recorder was still where Nonno had left it. He rewound the tape and pressed play. Nonno's voice was as clear as if he was in the room.

"The cafe was open every day including Sunday, when we opened in the morning. There was always something to do – cooking, making drinks, serving and cleaning.

Papà preserved food too. He made salami and cheese, and he pickled or dried everything under the sun – tomatoes, courgettes, green beans and even fruit, like peaches, pears, oranges. We had jars and jars of preserved food all stacked up in the attic and in the kitchen cupboards. We used to sell produce too, a bit like Mr Malewski does now.

Papà and Mamma cared about people, they really did. There were lots of customers 'on tick', as we used to say then, which meant that they didn't have to pay straight away, just when they could. It was a busy time. The mines all around the area were producing tons of coal – coal that was shipped down to Cardiff and Barry docks and sent all over the world. The miners often came into the cafe before and after their shift.

Papà never complained when the tables and chairs got dirty from the coal dust, because the miners were our best customers.

The thing I remember more than anything else was Papà working hard. He used to say to me that to finish the day and know that you'd filled it with hard work was the best feeling in the world.

It was around nineteen thirty-eight that Papà got a letter from Mario, his brother-in-law, back in his home town. There was trouble brewing in Italy – Benito Mussolini and his fascists were in power. Papà was worried as he was loyal to Italy but his life was here in Wales.

He telegraphed Mario and told him to come over with his sister – there was work and he'd be welcome. Mario sent a telegram back saying they had little money and Mussolini was restricting how many Italians could leave Italy. So Papà sent him another telegram with some money – 'Come over quickly. Whatever it takes.'

It was a few months later that Mario came with Zia, my aunt. She was Mimi's great-grandmother. By the time they arrived Papà hardly recognised them, they were so thin.

Mario told us they'd worked their way through France as they'd run out of money. I remember helping to cook the evening meal that day. Zia had tears in her eyes as

Papà brought the food to the table.

Mario spoke about how worried he was. See, Mussolini was getting friendly with Hitler, and if he went further Mario worried where that would leave their friends and relatives back in Italy. Papà told him they were safe here, and that they could help in the cafe. He laughed and said, 'Maybe one day you open your own cafe!'

Mario and Zia needed a room to themselves, so I gave them mine and moved up into the attic, ironically my room now. They all worked hard, and business was even better, but they didn't realise then what the future held. As it turned out they should have all stayed in Italy — and I mean all of us, including Papà, Mamma and me..."

There was silence, then Joe could hear Nonno making noises. He realised it was the moment he'd had the stroke. Joe stopped the tape. He stood up, feeling edgy, and had a sudden ache of hunger. He went downstairs.

NINE

Joe took out a pan and poured in some oil. He lit the hob just as Mam came in from the cafe. "What you doing?"

"Cooking, Mam."

"You don't have to, Joe, I'll knock up a—"

"I want to, Mam. I want to."

Joe hadn't a clue what he was doing as he'd never cooked a meal on his own. He decided to cut up some onions, but his eyes immediately began to water.

"Oh, you all right, love?"

"I'm not crying," said Joe. "Bloody onions!"

He dropped the diced onions into the pan and

they hissed loudly.

"I think the gas is too high," said Mam.

Joe lowered the heat and added minced beef.

Dad came in. "Cooking, are you, Joe?"

"Yes." Before Dad could say more, Joe added, "Cos I want to."

Dad and Mam went upstairs, while Joe struggled to decide what it was that he was actually cooking. The phone rang.

Joe tensed up as he answered, worried that it was more bad news. "Hello."

"*Hello... Is that Joe?*"

"Yes."

"*Gelato Joe! Is Mimi speaking.*"

Joe was irritated and wished he hadn't sent her the email. "Oh, hello."

"*I get your message,*" said Mimi. "*Poor Nonno. Is terrible.*"

Mam appeared. "Who is it?"

"Mimi from Italy."

Mam's brow knotted.

"*I want to come to see him,*" said Mimi. "*Perhaps I can 'elp. Yes?*"

"Oh, right... Sure," said Joe.

"*What is your address, please?*"

"It's Cafe Merelli. Number ten, the High Street,

Bryn Mawr, South Wales."

"*Again, please. Slowly.*"

Joe repeated it.

"*OK. I can come straight away – tomorrow.*"

Joe glanced at Mam. "Right. OK."

"*Goo'bye,*" said Mimi.

"Bye," said Joe.

"What was that all about?" Mam asked.

"That was Mimi."

"Yeah, I got that," said Mam.

Joe turned the wooden spoon in his hand. "I thought she should know what happened to Nonno. So I got on the laptop—"

"Did you explain he wasn't dead?"

"Mam! Course I did. What d'you think I said?"

"Well, what did she want the address for? Send flowers, is it?"

Joe stared at the table and tried to imagine a lovely meal that he'd cooked, all ready to eat. "She's coming."

"Coming!" Mam's eyes opened wide. "What, here?"

Before Joe could say anything he smelled burning. Dinner was ruined.

TEN

"Your cousin?" said Combi as they walked along the High Street.

"Yeah, from Italy," said Joe. "She's annoying."

"All cousins are annoying," said Combi. "Fact."

"Mam says I got to give up my bedroom and go up to Nonno's room."

"This cousin," said Combi. "She older or younger than you?"

"Older. Why?"

"Bad luck. See, legally she can order you around."

"Legally! You don't 'alf talk cack sometimes."

Combi shrugged. "I'm off to the Chicken Box."

"Don't rub it in," said Joe, just as a hand slapped on to his shoulder. He looked up to see Bonner towering over him.

"Bad about your gramps, Davis."

Bonner was a year above Joe and built like a buffalo. He had an explosion of curly black hair and always wore a fixed grin. Joe could never tell if he was just happy or teetering on insanity. "Had a stroke, I heard," he added.

"Yes," said Joe.

"Funny word, that – stroke." He gazed into the distance. "They should say something else, I reckon … like brain-melt. That would be better."

"No," said Joe. "It wouldn't."

Bonner's fixed grin dropped. "As you have troubles, I'll let that go." He walked away, followed by his gang skipping to keep up.

"Neanderthal turd," said Combi. "Joe. Come have some chicken with me."

Joe felt saliva fill his mouth at the thought. "I can't, Combi. I can't."

At the hospital Nonno listened as Mam explained about Mimi coming. Joe could see that his face was still half paralysed from the stroke. He spoke slowly and quietly. "It's nice that she's coming, Lucia."

"It's not convenient," said Mam. "I mean, what's she going to do here?"

"She's a good cook, Lucia," said Nonno. He looked at Joe. "Her great-grandmother came to the cafe a long time ago, during the war."

"Yeah, I heard about it on the tape you did, Nonno," said Joe. "I mean the one that was left in the tape recorder. It's really good."

"What tape?" asked Mam.

"The history of the cafe," he said.

Nonno's hand fell on to Joe's. "It's a long story. I'll tell you the rest ... when I'm feeling better, yeah?"

"Sure. Take it easy, Nonno."

When they got back to the cafe Joe decided to stay out and take a *passeggiata* on his own. He wandered across to the other side of the High Street. He gazed at the cafe in the dark and became overcome with sadness at the thought of it being closed and sold. He looked at the faded shopfront – *Cafe Merelli est.1929*.

He realised it wasn't far off a hundred years old. He imagined it lit up and full of customers and the sounds of merry-making on a cold winter's night. His imagination was interrupted by a text from Mam.

Come back, Joe. She's here!

ELEVEN

The back-door window was steamed up.

As Joe entered he smelled lovely herbs and spices. Someone was standing at the cooker, stirring the contents of a large frying pan. *That can't be Mimi,* he thought.

"Hello," he said.

She turned, and Joe sharply drew in his breath.

She was a young woman with long black hair and a straight fringe, framing her face. Her eyes were big and as dark as black olives, but there was a hint of sadness in them. Her lips were full and as red as chillies.

Joe's heart was thumping – she was prettier than anyone he'd ever seen before, and certainly not recognisable as the annoying girl he'd met when he was eight.

Mimi smiled and her eyes lost their sadness. Joe could hear beautiful music with a voice singing like an angel.

"*Ciao*, Joe," she said in a strong Italian accent, and she kissed him on both cheeks.

"Thanks," said Joe as he realised the music was coming from the CD player.

"I cook nice pasta," said Mimi. "I love to cook."

"Oh, OK... Where's my mam and dad?" asked Joe, wondering if he'd been left alone in the house. Mimi pointed upstairs.

"I ... go upstairs ... to see them," Joe said slowly.

"I understand English," said Mimi.

"Yeah, sorry."

"Hey, Joe," she said. "You still like the *gelato*?"

"Not so much," he replied, lying through his teeth.

Mimi laughed, and Joe went up to the lounge where he found Mam and Dad in conference.

"You met our guest, I take it?" said Mam.

Joe pointed down the stairs. "She's ... she's a woman!"

"Ten out of ten, Joe."

"Pretty, isn't she?" said Dad.

"Didn't notice," said Joe. He could still feel his heart beating, but convinced himself he'd rushed up the stairs too quickly.

"She's been getting on my nerves since she arrived," said Mam. "Taken over the place – '*I want to 'elp*'...'*I lav to cook*'. And we hardly know her, really."

"Well, she's definitely Italian," said Joe.

Mam groaned. "Oh, well, there we are then. I'm 'appy now."

Mimi was totally engrossed in the job of cooking as Joe laid the table. The lovely smell of the food made him ravenous.

Mimi brought a large saucepan to the table, and they sat down to dinner.

Joe sensed a strained atmosphere.

"Good of you to cook for us," said Dad.

"Oh, please, I *want* to cook," said Mimi.

Joe watched her dishing out the pasta. She grated Parmesan cheese on each plate, like he'd seen waiters do in restaurants.

"*Pasta Bolognese*," she said, as if someone had asked. "*Buon Appetito*."

When Joe tasted a mouthful he was amazed how delicious it was – a dense taste, better than any pasta he'd eaten before. Food was suddenly different – he felt as if his taste buds were doing the cha-cha-cha on *Strictly*.

"Oh, that's lovely," said Dad.

"You like, Joe?" asked Mimi.

"Yeah. It's... It's like restaurant food."

She laughed. "You go to restaurant very much?"

"Yes," he said, just as Mam said, "No."

"Joe, you're not confusing 'restaurants' with the Chicken Box?" Mam asked.

"No!" said Joe.

"What is Chicken Box?" asked Mimi.

"It's a takeaway – bottom-of-the-range chicken and chips," said Dad.

"Aye. You see leftovers on the pavement everywhere," said Mam. "Even pigeons give it a miss. Joe loves it."

"I do NOT!" said Joe.

Mam looked puzzled. "You and Combi eat it by the box-load."

"Who is Combi?" asked Mimi.

"He's a friend," said Joe. "Has a very poor diet." He continued to eat the pasta, which seemed to get better with every mouthful.

"Nonno was telling us that your great-grandma came 'ere in the war," said Joe, in an effort to keep the conversation going.

"Yes," said Mimi. "She die a long time before I was born. But I remember my grandmother tell me she came here."

"Forgive me for asking," said Mam, "but how is it you've come to see my dad after so long?"

Joe couldn't believe Mam's nerve. Mimi appeared quite surprised. "I was worried about Nonno. I want to 'elp – I can cook..."

"Well, if you keep making food like this you can stay as long as you like," said Dad with a chuckle. Then he looked at Mam and his laughter fizzled out.

As they carried on eating Joe sneaked a glance at Mimi, now and again, as he didn't want to stare. She ate with great intensity, like nothing else mattered. He thought she was so beautiful – beautiful like he'd seen in magazines and films.

After dinner Joe took Mimi into the cafe and switched on the lights. Mam stood at the doorway. "This is Cafe Merelli," Joe said with pride.

Mimi gazed around the cafe and her brow immediately crinkled, as if she was seeing something she'd never seen before. She ran her finger across the glass cabinet and examined it. "Is dirty," she said. "You need 'elp with cleaning too, no?"

Joe saw Mam's cheeks flush. "I'll sack the cleaner."

"We haven't got a cleaner," he said.

Mam stared at him. "Oh, yeah, that's right."

Mimi was now prodding at a taped repair on one of the booth seats. She looked around and Joe noticed a slight shake of her head.

"We get good breakfast trade in the mornings," he said. "Nonno usually cooks it."

"I can cook it," said Mimi.

Joe glanced at Mam. "Sausage, egg, bacon, beans and fried tomato," she said.

"For breakfast?" said Mimi.

"Yes," said Joe.

Mimi blew out her cheeks.

Mam switched out the lights. "Right. Show's over."

Joe took the last of his clothes up to Nonno's room and put them away. He gazed at the selection of opera CDs and decided to play one of them. It was called *Madam Butterfly*. The music was lovely.

There was a knock at the door.

"Yeah."

Dad popped his head in. "Got yourself all sorted, Joe?"

"Yeah. Tidy."

"What you listening to?" Dad asked.

"*Madam Butterfly*."

"Didn't know you liked opera, Joe."

"All Italians like opera, Dad."

"Oh, OK. Night night."

There was a puzzled expression on his dad's face as he shut the door.

Joe started to read the story of the opera as the music washed over him.

TWELVE

Joe didn't like the way his shirt buttons pulled, as if they'd pop at any moment. He stood in front of the mirror and turned sideways. His belly overhung his trousers.

"Growing too fast," he said to himself.

As he made his way downstairs he heard an argument coming from the kitchen. He found Mimi facing Mam, who was looking flustered.

"You cook the bacon again in the microwave?" Mimi said. "After you fry?"

"Yes," said Mam.

"Why?"

"Saves money. No waste."

Mimi pulled a face. "'Orrible."

"Well, the customers don't seem to mind!"

"Is too much frying," said Mimi. "And eggs I like to cook in butter, not oil, or I can poach them."

"Poached?" said Mam.

"Is like boiled," said Mimi.

"I know what poached is!" said Mam as she turned and went back into the cafe.

Mimi looked at Joe. "I only try to 'elp."

"I know," he said. "She's stressed."

Joe noticed the difference in the food straight away as he took the orders out to their regulars – the breakfasts were clean and simple, and there was no sign of oil or grease.

"What's this?" asked Mr Kempski, one of a group of Polish workmen.

"Our new breakfast," said Joe. "Cooked by a proper..." He glanced at Mam. "All fresh, it is. Any extra tea or coffee, just ask. No extra."

Mimi watched from the doorway as the customers tucked in. Joe could see the surprised expressions on their faces as they ate the food.

Joe had his breakfast in the cafe as usual. The scrambled eggs that Mimi had cooked were much tastier, and they even looked more yellow.

Vaughan entered. "I heard the news about Mr Merelli," he said. "Gutted, I was. I wish him a speedy recovery."

"Thank you," said Mam.

Mimi came out of the kitchen and Vaughan's eyes opened like saucers. Joe introduced him to her.

"Oh, now," he said. "You're b'utiful. Welcome to Wales."

"Thank you," said Mimi.

The Polish workmen went up to the counter to pay. "Same price, less food," Mr Kempski said to Mam.

"Trying out a new cook," she said.

"Well, I'm still hungry," he said as he left.

Mimi came over to Joe. "You like it?"

Joe could see Mam was listening. "It was very tasty," he said with a smile, just as Combi walked into the cafe holding a can of Coke and a half-eaten sausage roll.

"You coming, Joe?"

"Hello," said Mimi.

Combi's mouth dropped open, displaying his mashed-up sausage roll. Joe stood up and stepped between him and Mimi. "I'll catch you later, Combi. I'm busy."

Combi peered around Joe. "Hello. You must be

49

Joe's cousin," he said.

"Yes."

"I'm Joe's mate." He held out his can to Mimi. "Want some Coke?"

"That's not a suitable breakfast drink!" Joe said as he ushered him towards the door.

"Funny, innit?" he heard Vaughan say. "If you mashed all the food together on the plate you wouldn't want it, would you? But once it's in your stomach…"

Joe was about to apologise to Mimi when he saw she was laughing.

"See you later," he called, dragging Combi outside.

"She's stonking, isn't she?" said Combi.

Joe didn't like the way he was staring at Mimi. "Didn't notice," he said.

"Didn't notice!" said Combi in surprise. "Has she got a boyfriend?"

"No idea," said Joe, hurrying him along.

THIRTEEN

After school Joe went to see Nonno at the hospital and found Mam and Mimi at his bedside. Joe thought Nonno was looking much better.

"I don't see the point," said Mam.

"What's going on?" Joe asked.

"I want to make food for the cafe," said Mimi.

"We do make food."

"No," she said. "Proper Italian food."

"Charming," said Mam.

"It's a good idea," said Joe.

"There's no point," Mam replied. "There'll be no takers. It's a High Street that's dying."

Nonno raised his hand. "Lucia," he said softly. "Let her try, please. Just for a while."

They sat in uncomfortable silence, until Mam said, "Joe. Can you go back to the cafe with Mimi – I want to talk to Nonno, and your dad's holding the fort on his own."

He knew Mam meant business so he didn't argue, even though he wanted to talk to Nonno himself.

It was raining by the time they got back, and Gwen was the only one left in the cafe, waiting for her bus home. Joe tried to look authoritative behind the counter as Mimi wandered around the cafe. He smiled at Gwen. "I'll give you a shout if the bus comes."

"Thanks Joe," she said. "I've heard that in Cardiff there's displays at bus stops that tell you when the next bus is coming. I'll be long gone before that luxury gets to the Mawr."

Mimi fiddled with the old espresso coffee machine behind the counter.

"Doesn't work," said Joe.

"How long is it broken?"

"Years."

"What if a customer want coffee?" she asked.

"We give 'em instant," said Joe, and he saw her grimace.

She wandered over to the old photographs of the cafe on the wall.

"You're very pretty," Gwen said to her.

"Thank you," she replied with a smile.

Joe went and stood beside her. "That's Nonno in nineteen fifty-three," he said, pointing at the photo.

Mimi nodded.

"There's the bus," said Gwen. "Oh, stop it for me, Joe. Please."

"Sure!"

Joe ran outside and dramatically waved at the bus. He hoped Mimi was watching. The bus pulled up and Joe checked back to see Mimi emerge from the cafe holding an umbrella over Gwen. "She's just coming," he said to the driver.

"Big taxi, am I?" the driver replied.

"What kept you?" Gwen said as she got on.

"I was having a nap round the corner."

"I bet you were, an' all!"

They started arguing with each other, until Joe said to the driver, "Would you like a cup of tea or coffee?"

"What?"

"I'll get you a tea, from the cafe."

"This a joke?"

Joe was amazed at himself – it was almost as if someone else had spoken. "No joke – if you text the cafe when you're near we'll give you a free cuppa. Then people can wait inside, see?"

The passengers were watching as the rain was noisily peppering the roof of the bus. "Is this straight up?" the driver asked.

"It's brilliant," said Gwen. "We can wait in the cafe, out of the cold and rain, and we won't be complaining to you, will we?"

The driver looked from Gwen to Joe. "A free cuppa?"

"And you can tell the other drivers the same thing," said Joe.

The bus doors closed with a hiss. "You're on."

FOURTEEN

Joe picked out one of Nonno's CDs. It was called *La Bohème* by Puccini. The opera was lovely, especially as one of the main characters was called Mimi, and the tenor, Rodolfo, falls in love with her. By the time he got to the end of the second act he could smell cooking from downstairs.

Mimi was busy in the kitchen as he entered.

"You listen to *La Bohème*?" she asked.

"Yes," said Joe.

She threw back her head and sang a piece that Joe had just heard. It made him laugh, and she had a lovely voice.

"You like to cook, Joe?"

He realised it was something he'd like to do even if he didn't know how. "Yes," he said as he watched Mimi at the cooker. She was confidently chopping ingredients – it was noisy and exciting. She seemed in complete control.

"You're like Jamie Oliver," he said.

Mimi's eyebrow shot up. "I look like Jamie Oliver?"

"No!" said Joe. "Not at all. Just the way..." He pointed at her chopping.

She laughed.

"Can you cook pizza?" Joe asked.

Mimi pulled a face. "Yes, is simple, but pizza is not a proper meal."

"Why not?"

"The people from Napoli invent pizza many, many years ago – was just a snack."

"It's still lovely," said Joe licking his lips.

"Does the cafe open in the evening?" Mimi asked.

"No."

"Why?"

Joe tried to pull the corners of his mouth down, but only succeeded in raising his eyebrows. Mimi was looking at him with a puzzled expression, so Joe said, "I don't know."

* * *

At dinner Mam and Dad were quiet. The food was risotto with courgettes and Dolcelatte cheese.

"Delicious," Joe said in an effort to lift the atmosphere.

"Yummy," said Dad. "I heard about your idea for the bus drivers, Joe. Very enterprising."

"Bravo," said Mimi. "Is fantastic – no, Lucia?"

"A bus stop with chairs, we'll be," said Mam.

The silence continued until Mimi said, "I would like to fix the espresso machine."

"Why?" asked Mam.

"So we can have fresh coffee," she said. "No instant."

"'Orrible, I suppose?" said Mam.

Mimi pulled a face. "Yes."

"Joe," said Mam. "Have you heard anyone complain about our coffee?"

He glanced at Mimi waiting on his word. "No."

"I would like to fix anyway," said Mimi.

"You tried to give our customers a different breakfast and they weren't bothered," said Mam. "The same will happen if you offer them proper coffee, but if you want to fix it go ahead."

After dinner Joe helped Mimi begin on the espresso machine. She tied up her hair, which he thought made her look even prettier. Mimi used some of

Dad's tools, and grappled to take the outer casing off. When it came away she said, "*Mamma mia! È messo malissimo!*"

"What does *malissimo* mean?" Joe asked.

"*Male* is bad. *Malissimo* is very bad. In Italian you put *issimo* to make more. Like ... *bello – bellissimo*, mean beautiful, very beautiful, or *brutto – bruttissimo*, mean ugly, very ugly."

"I get it."

Joe could see that a lot of the inner parts of the coffee machine had calcified. He marvelled at Mimi's intensity when she was focused on the job at hand, like when she was cooking. She stared at the machine and muttered in Italian.

"Can you fix it?" Joe asked.

She turned to him and said, "Yes. I fix."

Joe gazed into her beautiful dark eyes. He felt his heart bang inside his chest, as if it was telling him he was in love – in love big time.

FIFTEEN

Next morning Joe was up early. He read the instructions on the back of the tube of hair gel and then looked at himself in the mirror. He smoothed the gel into his hair and began to comb it through. It made him look older, which pleased him.

He tried sweeping his hair back, ignoring his usual side parting.

He peered at himself. "Look like a vampire," he said. He ruffled his hair to try and make it look casual, but it stayed up in spikes. "Boy band now." He growled with frustration, so he combed in his usual parting and went downstairs.

"What you done to your hair?" Mam asked, which sent a tremor of embarrassment through Joe.

"It was all... So I put on hair gel."

"Didn't know you had hair gel."

Joe was going to pull the corners of his mouth down, but decided on a shrug instead. The cafe doorbell rang as the door opened. A woman stood in the entrance. "That right, what I've heard? You'll tell us when the bus is due?"

"That's right," said Joe. "Come into the warm and we'll let you know. Cup of tea or coffee?"

"Go on then – tea, please."

He felt proud, and grinned at Mam as he began to prepare the drink.

"Very good, Joe," she said.

The bell clanged again and Bonner filled the doorway – his gang were bunched up behind as if they were tethered to him. "Where is she then?"

"Who?" Joe asked, pretending he didn't know.

"This girl I've heard about – Mimi. Where is she?"

"She's out."

"No she isn't," said Mam. "Mimi!" she called through to the kitchen. "Someone to see you."

When Mimi came into the cafe Joe saw Bonner's mouth drop open. "Oh, where you been all my life, love?" he said as he offered her his hulk-like hand.

"I'm Bonner – scrum half for Bryn Mawr School rugby and man about town."

Mimi laughed. Joe was uneasy, as the other boys were nudging each other and staring with popping eyes. Combi walked in, eating a doughnut. "Told you she was stonking," he said to the boys.

"Are you at school with Joe?" Mimi asked Bonner.

Bonner glanced down as if noticing Joe for the first time. "Oh, aye," he said. "We could use Joe in the front row at the rugby club – always need boys with a bit of weight on 'em." He slapped a hand on Joe's shoulder and Joe winced.

"Rugby," said Mam. "Now there's a good idea for you to get trim, Joe."

"I'll look after him, Mrs Davis," said Bonner with a second slap on his shoulder. Joe wasn't happy at all, especially when Combi pointed at him and said in front of everyone, "What you done to your hair, Joe?"

SIXTEEN

Joe went to visit Nonno after school and found him alone.

"How is your mam?" Nonno asked quietly. "You know, with Mimi, I mean."

"Mimi's getting on her nerves, to be honest, Nonno."

"Do you like Mimi?" he asked.

Joe shrugged stiffly and stared down at his lap. He didn't want to give away how he felt about her. "She wants to fix the espresso machine so we can do fresh coffee. She said it was a sin to offer instant."

"She's right," said Nonno. "Shame on us. The old

San Marco hasn't worked in years. Mimi came to see me today and brought me food. Oh, it was lovely, Joe. Much better than the hospital lunch. And she told me about your idea – people waiting for the bus in the cafe." Nonno smiled with only half of his mouth – a half-smile. "But I don't want your mam to feel left out, Joe. It's difficult for her."

Joe nodded. "I wish you were back at the cafe."

"Me too."

"Listening to your opera, I am, Nonno."

"Good," he said. "Why don't you bring me the tape recorder, Joe. I want to continue the story – it will keep me occupied."

Joe was pleased. "OK, Nonno."

On the way home Joe bumped into Combi. "Everyone's talking about Mimi," he said.

Joe guessed everyone was talking about her, but he didn't want to know. "I'm busy."

"Where you off?" Combi asked.

"Bryn Mawr library."

When Joe entered he realised he wasn't even a member, and so he asked for a library card.

"What you getting?" asked Combi as Joe filled out the form.

"Cookery books."

"Cookery books?"

"Yeah. Y'know – recipes for meals and how to cook them. Haven't you ever cooked a meal, Combi?"

"Yeah ... sandwich."

"That's not cooking."

"It was toasted, all right!"

Joe went to the cookery section and found lots of Italian cookery books. He selected three and then went on to the language section for an Italian phrase book. He was pleased to find one with a whole section on food and restaurants.

"What's all this about then?" asked Combi.

"I'm Italian and I wanna cook."

Joe ignored Combi's tutting and took the books to be checked out.

"Want a hand carrying them to the cafe?" Combi asked as they left the library.

"No, thanks."

"Sure now?"

"*No*, thanks."

"I'll pop by the caff later," said Combi.

"What for?"

Combi shrugged, but Joe knew why, and his irritation was growing.

SEVENTEEN

Joe slipped in the back way and took the books up to his room. Then he went back down and entered the cafe. Mam was standing at the counter. "'Lo, Mam."

"Hello."

Joe saw a large group of boys filling two of the booths. It puzzled him, as boys didn't come into the cafe after school – they usually gathered outside the Chicken Box. Combi was among them and gave Joe a wave.

"What's all this about?" whispered Joe with a nod towards the boys.

"I wonder?" said Mam.

"Where's Mimi then?" asked Combi, just as Mam's mobile phone bleeped.

"Bus to Aber arriving," she said aloud. Some of the other customers got to their feet and went out. "Can someone take a tea to the driver?"

Vaughan was left behind with the group of boys. "Lively now, this place."

"Aye – lively bus stop," said Mam. "Wonderful."

Joe heard a door slam and someone coming down from upstairs.

Mimi entered the cafe.

"Hello," said Joe.

The boys stood up, and some of them gasped.

"I go out," said Mimi. "You come with me, Joe?"

"Sure." He glanced at the boys. "D'you think you can manage, Mam?"

"Just about," she replied. "I've always got your mobile in an emergency."

"I'll get my coat."

Joe darted into the kitchen, but by the time he came back into the cafe Mimi was surrounded by the boys.

"From Italy, she is," said Combi. "Joe's cousin."

Joe pushed his way into the middle of the group. "Give her some air!"

"Combi," said Mimi. "Would you like to come to

dinner tonight?"

The clamour of the boys came to a halt.

"Why?" asked Joe.

"He's your friend," said Mimi. "In Italy we invite friends for dinner."

"Why not?" said Combi with a grin at Joe. "I'll have to ask my mam, but she'll be cool."

Joe went out with Mimi. He loved the way she confidently walked along the street with her head back, her hair bouncing with each step as if it was happy to be on her head. Unfortunately for Joe the herd of boys closed around them like a rugby maul, and by the time they arrived outside the Chicken Box they were surrounded by children.

"You're Mimi, aren't you?" said Cathy Jones.

"Yes."

"We've 'eard about you."

"She's gorgeous," another girl said, and there were mutterings of agreement. "Lovely hair." "Fab'lous eyes." "Got any tattoos?"

Ryan Jenkins offered her his box of chips. "Want one?"

Mimi picked up a chip, examined it and tasted it. Her nose screwed up. "Is greasy and soft."

"I know," said Ryan. "Lovely, in' they?"

"This food is very, very bad for you," said Mimi.

Joe nodded in agreement. "Jamie Oliver," he said.

"Say something in Italian," Cathy said to Mimi.

"*Mi chiamo Mimi. Piacere di conoscerti.*"

"What's that mean?"

"My name's Mimi. I'm happy to meet you," said Joe.

"Your name's not Mimi!" said Ryan, and the others laughed.

"She doesn't look anything like you, Joe," said Cathy.

They all peered at him, looking for some similarity, and time seemed to stand still.

"Mr Malewski's," Mimi said, gazing across the road. "What is this?"

"Shop for people from Poland," said Combi. "And places like that."

Mimi crossed the road, and the children went with her.

"Dinner then," Combi said to Joe as they followed.

"If your mam lets you."

"She been asking about me then?"

"Who?"

"Mimi."

Joe stopped. "Asking about you? No, she hasn't."

"You sure?"

Joe was suddenly pulled round and found himself

face to face with Bonner. "Davis! I want Mimi's mobile number. I'm inviting her to the rugby on Saturday."

"I don't think she's got one," he said as he saw Mimi walk into Mr Malewski's.

"Don't give me that," said Bonner. "My mam's cat's got a mobile. What's her number?"

"I don't know."

"Trying to keep her to yourself, aren't you?"

"No."

"He is, Bon," said Combi. "Mimi just invited me to dinner and he's jealous."

Bonner glared at him. "She invited you to dinner?"

"Yeah."

"How come?"

Combi shrugged. "Maybe she fancies me."

Bonner roared with laughter. "Good one." He clapped a hand on Combi's shoulder. "I tell you, when Mimi sees me in the rugby match, brushing players off like crumbs, she'll faint – mark my words."

Joe was worried as he watched him go.

"She wouldn't give Bonner the time of day," said Combi. "Would she?"

"No," said Joe as he rushed to catch up with Mimi, but he wasn't sure.

EIGHTEEN

The children had stayed outside the shop as Joe entered Malewski's Emporium. He saw Mimi in front of a fridge with a small girl. "What you looking for?" he asked.

"I'm interested in different food, Joe," said Mimi. "And different ingredients."

"Never been in here before," said Joe looking around.

"Why?" the girl asked.

Joe shrugged. "It's for Polish people, innit?"

"Food is food, Joe," said Mimi. "This is Marta. She work here."

"Works here?"

"After school I help out," said Marta. "Mr Malewski is my dad, and he told me when I am eighteen," she held up seven fingers, "in seven years' time, I can be deputy manager." She winked at Joe.

"What is this?" asked Mimi, holding up a jar.

"Pickled cabbage," said Marta.

"Lovely," said Mimi.

"You want to buy or look?"

Joe turned and saw a man holding several boxes. He muttered something in Polish to Marta, who threw her hands in the air and said something back. The young man glared at Mimi. "You Polish?"

"No. Italian."

"No Italian food here."

"This is my brother, Dariusz," said Marta. "He'll work for me when I take over."

Dariusz laughed, revealing a gold tooth. Joe thought he was rude, but he couldn't help noticing his penetrating blue eyes, and that his shirt sleeves were rolled up high, revealing muscular, tattooed arms.

"Do you have just Polish food?" Mimi asked.

"No," said Marta. "We have food from Russia, Bulgaria, Lithuania, Romania..."

"Why not Italian food?"

"Italian food is everywhere – any supermarket," Dariusz said. He moved closer to Mimi – too close for Joe's liking.

Marta stepped between them. "People come here because they miss things from their country, you understand?" she said. "They pay money, they go away happy and they come back when they feel sad and miss their country again. Good business, yes?" She grinned.

"Very good," said Mimi.

Joe tried to pull the corners of his mouth down but only managed to raise his eyebrows again. He needed practice.

"Hello, Joe," said Mr Malewski, coming through from the back of the shop. "I heard about Mr Merelli. How is he?"

"Getting better," said Joe.

"Good. Good."

Marta began speaking in Polish again. Mr Malewski nodded. Marta took a vacuum-packed sausage out of the fridge and handed it to Mimi. "*Kabanos* – very good Polish sausage."

"How much?" Mimi asked.

"Free sample," said Mr Malewski. "For Mr Merelli and you, pretty lady."

"Thank you," said Mimi.

"Come back soon and try something else," said Marta. "One day this shop will be mine." Mr Malewski laughed, as Marta and Dariusz began arguing.

Joe and Mimi returned to the cafe with the crowd of children still surrounding them, like a flock of sheep. Joe thought how cool and grown up Mimi seemed, and he wondered if many women married men younger than themselves.

"How old are you, Mimi?" Combi asked as if he'd read Joe's mind.

"Twenty," said Mimi. "Why?"

"I thought you were older," said Combi.

Joe stopped him as Mimi walked on. "That was rude."

"No," said Combi. "It's rude when you say that to old women, like our mams, but it's a compliment to young women – fact."

"*Crappissimo!*" said Joe.

"What?"

"You add *issimo* to the end of a word in Italian to make it bigger."

He saw that Mimi was about to go back into the cafe and ran ahead.

When he entered he quickly shut the cafe door. "We're closed," he shouted at the children outside.

"Joe! There's another half-hour yet," said Mam.

"They're just time-wasters," said Joe as he locked the door. "We'll have an early night."

"See you for dinner," Combi said through the window.

Joe pulled the blind down.

"What was Mimi doing over in Malewski's?" asked Mam.

"She's interested in food."

"What, even Polish food?"

"Yeah, Mam. What's wrong with that?"

Joe went upstairs to start reading his books.

NINETEEN

Joe's mouth watered as he skimmed through the recipes in the cookery books. He could even smell lovely herbs and spices, but then realised Mimi must be cooking. He decided now was the time to ask.

Downstairs he found her working intensively in the kitchen as usual. She seemed to be in the zone, so Joe began to set the table for dinner. "Mimi..."

She replied with a noise.

"I used to watch Nonno cook..."

"Is he good?"

"Yes, very."

Mimi furiously cut up an onion and Joe had to

shout to be heard. "Will you teach me to cook?"

Mimi stopped and turned. "Sure, Joe," she said with a smile. "A pasta sauce is easy," she said. "You fry chopped onion, garlic and add a tin of tomatoes. Then you put in whatever you want – meat, fish ... or peas, courgettes, mushrooms, and always salt, pepper and herbs."

She talked as she cooked.

Joe noticed how much she used her hands to make gestures as she spoke. One, in particular, he noticed she used a lot – she held the ends of her fingers and thumb together and moved her hand back and forth, as if shaking something. "Why d'you make this gesture with your hand?" he asked, demonstrating what he'd seen.

"All Italians use hands when they speak. This one," she said, repeating the gesture with her fingers held together, "can mean, *'Can you believe it?'* or *'What you talking about?'*"

Joe laughed, because as she spoke the gesture seemed to fit, like she was emphasising what she was saying. The back doorbell rang.

Joe opened the door to see Combi holding a bunch of flowers – he seemed different in some way. "What you done to your hair?"

"Nothing," said Combi as he walked past Joe and

handed Mimi the flowers. "For you."

"Oh, thank you." Mimi kissed him on both cheeks.

Joe had never seen Combi blush so much since the time his trousers had ripped when he'd bent over to pick up a Bounty bar.

"Let me take your coat," Joe said.

"Take my coat where?"

Joe noticed Combi was staring at Mimi with a grin on his face, as if he was looking at a box of puppies. "So ... how's it going?" Joe asked.

"Fine," Combi replied without even looking at him.

"Wanna game on the console?" Joe said to distract him.

"No. You're all right," said Combi. "I'll stay here."

Joe was hit by a wave of irritation, as strong as the smell of frying onions. He had a rival for Mimi, and his rival was his best mate.

TWENTY

Everyone sat down for dinner, and Mimi began to serve out portions. The plates were passed around the table. "Drink, Combi?" Dad asked.

"Coke, please."

"Actually," said Joe, "water or wine complements food better."

"Got that from a book, did you?" said Combi as a plate of food was put before him. "What's this?"

"Chicken escalope in breadcrumbs," said Mimi.

Combi prodded the vegetable on the side. "But what's this – onion?"

"Fennel," said Mimi.

"What's fennel?" he asked.

Joe tutted.

"Well, what *is* fennel?" Combi asked him.

Joe panicked. "It's fennel, isn't it?"

"We've never had it," Mam said to Mimi.

"*I* have!" said Joe.

"What's it taste like then?" Mam asked.

Joe didn't know, but before he could answer Combi said, "Liquorice! Tastes like liquorice. How weird is that?"

Joe tasted some quickly. "Not liquorice. Aniseed."

"You like it, Combi?" Mimi asked.

"Yeah. It's as lovely as you are," he said.

"Oh, he's a charmer," said Mam.

Joe had to suppress a groan. "*È molto buono*," he said to Mimi. "*Buonissimo.*"

"You speak Italian, Joe!" she said.

"*Un poco*," he replied. "*È pieno … di sapore. Saporissimo!*"

"What's that mean?" asked Combi.

"It's full of taste," said Joe.

"Yeah, like Coke," Combi replied.

"Oh, by the way, Joe," said Mam. "I signed you up for rugby training."

"What? I don't want to."

"Oh, come on," said Mam. "It'll do you good. Mr

Carter said he's always glad of new recruits. It's on Saturday, half past two at the Bryn Mawr ground."

"Maybe you'll be a natural," said Dad. "Future Welsh International."

"I'll sell tickets," said Combi, and Joe gave him a kick under the table.

"Ah yes. Rugby," said Mimi. "Bonner – he ask me to go to watch him."

"It'll be dead boring," said Combi. "Boring-*issimo*!" he added with a grin at Joe.

"If Joe play, I go," said Mimi.

"OK, I'll take you," said Combi.

"No need," said Joe.

"I'd *like* to," said Combi.

They glared at each other.

"Combi, what do you like to eat at home?" asked Mimi.

"It varies," he said, lacing his fingers together. "But generally speaking, Mimi, fish fingers are my favourite."

"Fish ... fingers?" she repeated. "What is this?"

"Fish in breadcrumbs," said Dad.

"Very poor-quality food," added Joe.

"How d'you mean, 'poor quality'?" Combi asked.

"Well, they're not as nice as proper fish, are they?" said Joe.

"Yes, they are – no slimy skin. I love a fish finger sandwich."

"Fish ... finger ... sandwich," Mimi repeated.

"*We* have fish fingers," said Mam. "Never heard you complain, Joe."

"Not very often," Joe said to Mimi. "Maybe when Nonno's not cooking."

"Thanks, Joe," said Mam. "So when I've seen you holding out your plate for more you were forcing yourself, were you?"

Combi pointed at him. "Ha!"

"Nonno asked me to bring him the tape recorder," said Joe, to change the subject.

"What for?" asked Mam.

"He wants to carry on telling our history, Mam – the history of Cafe Merelli."

"Joe. Can you join the real world!" said Mam. "He's just had a stroke!"

"He *wants* to do it," said Joe. "Said it would help him. He's bored at the hospital."

"Do him good, love," said Dad. "Occupation – that's the key."

Mam sighed. "Take him the tape recorder but don't hassle him, Joe."

They went back to eating. Joe glanced at Mimi. He had found discouraging results on the

Internet about women with younger men – they were called horrible things like "cradle snatchers", and the men "toy boys". He noticed Combi staring at her again.

"Combi. D'you know *Rigoletto?*" he asked to distract him.

"Video game, is it?"

"No. It's an opera by Verdi. Dead good."

Combi rolled his eyes.

"Specially when Rigoletto's daughter gets abducted," said Joe. "They take her for a laugh, cos they think she's his girlfriend, see, but she's his daughter really and he keeps her hidden away."

"Sounds sick-*issimo*," said Combi.

Joe shook his head. "It's not. It's opera."

"By the way, Mimi," said Mam. "How's your papà and mamma?"

"Mamma is OK. She do little sewing for people, little cleaning – you know?"

"And papà?"

"Gone," said Mimi.

"Dead?"

"No. He met a dancer from Rome and he go."

"That's awful."

"Yes. Bad man," said Mimi. "And she not even a good dancer."

Mam shook her head.

Dad quickly got to his feet. "Joe, Combi, give us a hand with the dishes."

TWENTY ONE

Nonno was asleep when Joe got to the hospital ward, so he placed the tape recorder by his bed and wrote a note. *Take your time, Nonno. Just when you feel like it. Love Joe x.*

By the time he got back to the High Street it was dark – only Malewski's and the betting shop were still open. As he walked past the cafe he spotted Mimi, with her hair tied up, working on the espresso machine. Joe waved at her, but she didn't see him as she was totally engrossed in the job.

He ran round to the alley and into the backyard of the cafe. He was out of breath when he entered the kitchen and took off his coat. He checked his hair in the mirror, and entered the cafe as casually as he could.

"Hello," he said. "Want a hand?"

"Yes, you can clean this," she said, and handed him a part from inside the machine that was covered with calcium deposit.

Joe rolled up his sleeves and began to scrub it. He glanced at his biceps, but he was disappointed by how flabby they seemed. He thought Mimi was even more beautiful in the light reflecting off the shiny espresso machine, yet she seemed sad. "Is everything OK, Mimi?"

She turned to him and a strand of her hair dropped down. "Is nothing."

Joe thought about her father going off with a dancer. "I'd like to know," he said. "I mean... Families, eh?"

Mimi smiled and stroked his cheek. Joe's face became hot, as if her hand had magic powers. "Is it because you miss Italy?" he asked.

"Yes, a little, but ... this place make me sad, Joe."

"What, the cafe?"

She nodded. "I speak to Nonno at the hospital and he tell me how the cafe was, long ago. A cafe is like a person, Joe – they are all different. Some cafe is relaxed, some are ... how you say..." She made a snooty expression.

"Posh?"

"Yes. Some cafe is 'appy, but this one ... this one is sad."

Joe gazed around and realised that she was right.

"In Italy," she said. "Everyone love the cafe, or the restaurant – they meet and talk, but not here, and it make me feel sad."

"Is there ... is there someone, back in Italy?" Joe asked, desperate to know. "I mean ... like a boyfriend?"

"No," said Mimi. "But once..."

"Yes?" said Joe.

An odd expression passed over Mimi's face, like she was seeing through the walls. "My town have a festival of all local food," she said. "Sausage, pasta, cheese, bread, everything. And they cook too – everybody sharing and tasting. Is fantastic, Joe. There was a young man, cooking fresh tomatoes. I ask him what he make. He say to me 'a sauce' – but he no even look at me ... *antipatico*."

"Anti-what?"

"*Antipatico* – mean not nice or rude. He cook and taste, and cook and taste. And then he mix the sauce with the pasta and then serve it for people to try. So I taste."

"And?"

"Oh." She gathered the ends of her fingers and kissed them. "It was beautiful, and so simple, Joe. Fantastic. I look at him and he look at me ... then ... *PATTACRACK!*"

"What?"

"When I look in his eyes, I hear *PATTACRACK!*" said Mimi, with her eyes popping wide open. "Like thunder."

"Was he good-looking?"

Mimi pulled the corners of her mouth down. "Not really – big nose, big ears." She laughed. "But this is not important, Joe – his food. *Mamma mia!*"

"Then what happened?"

"My friends take me away to try other food, and when I go back, he was gone."

"But he must have been a local boy," said Joe.

Mimi shook her head. "I go to see the pasta maker the next day. I pretend I want to buy his pasta. I ask about the man who cook the sauce. He say, 'Ah, Giovanni? He go back to Naples.' Is like he vanish, Joe, like the taste of his sauce – beautiful, but gone." She stared out of the window as if she might catch sight of him.

"Didn't you go to Naples to try and find him?" Joe asked.

"I couldn't. Mamma needed me, and I had no

money." She gazed at him and tilted her head. "You ever look in someone's eyes, Joe, and hear thunder?"

"Not thunder," he said. "Heard music once."

There was a knock at the window. Joe saw a smartly dressed young man, and for a moment he wondered if it was Giovanni, or a new admirer of Mimi's. "We're closed," he said, though he thought it was pretty obvious.

"I've got an appointment with Mrs Davis," the man said from outside. "I'm the estate agent."

Joe opened the kitchen door and shouted upstairs. "Mam! Bloke outside – says he's an estate agent to see you."

"Let him in, Joe."

He went around the counter and began to unlock the cafe door. The man came in and brushed the rain off himself. "Shocker," he said. He looked around the cafe. "Well, this is retro."

"Good evening," said Mam as she entered. "You must be Mr Rawlings from the estate agent's."

Joe felt annoyed. "Mam, d'you tell Nonno this guy was coming?"

"D'you mind, Joe." She turned to the man and said, "Please follow me and I'll show you the premises."

"She's selling it," said Joe as Mam and the estate agent went upstairs.

"But you knew this, no?" said Mimi.

"Yes, but not straight away. Not while Nonno's still in hospital." He gazed at the two black-and-white photographs on the wall. "Not now."

"Poor Joe," said Mimi, touching his arm, but Joe realised that no one else cared – not like he did.

TWENTY TWO

Joe went straight to the hospital after school and told Nonno about the estate agent.

"You got to remember, Joe," said Nonno. "The cafe is your mam's. Look at the state I'm in – I can't help now."

"But Mimi's here to help."

"Only for a little while," said Nonno. "I know what you think, Joe, but there's something you need to realise – the cafe is our family business, but I gave it to your mam when it was already struggling. What kind of inheritance is that? Sure, I hoped that something would change, but it's not her fault. The lunch trade went when the mines closed down, then more recently the car factory. People don't eat out, Joe, not around here. Now your mam wants to sell. How can I stand in her way?"

Nonno's face was drawn and sad. "I suppose so," said Joe.

"I did more of the story for you," said Nonno, holding up a cassette tape.

Joe went straight up to his room when he got back.

"I remember the day that Hitler invaded Poland in nineteen thirty-nine. Papà and Mario were worried because Britain and France declared war against Germany, but Italy and Mussolini did nothing. It was a very tense time. Britain was at war. Everyone was nervous – Mussolini thought that Hitler was doing well and he didn't want to be left out. Then Hitler invaded France, and that was when we were really worried.

I think Papà knew what was coming and he started stock-piling provisions. He was preserving food round the clock – drying and storing beans, corn and potatoes. One day I was helping him as he was salting some fish, so that it would keep. 'What's going to happen, Papà?' I asked.

He stopped and stared at me, like he was deciding

whether I was big enough to be told. 'Italy will join Germany and declare war against Britain.'

'No, Papà,' I said. 'Mussolini is not that stupid.'

It was only two days later, very early in the morning, that I heard the knocking all the way up in the attic. It was an angry knocking, and I just knew something bad was happening.

PC Williams and an army officer came into the kitchen at the back of the cafe. I remember PC Williams just kept saying, 'Sorry, Mr Merelli.'

The army officer explained that because Mussolini had joined Hitler and Germany, the British government had decided to intern all enemy aliens. I'll never forget those words – enemy aliens.

Papà was confused, so the police officer put it in plain terms. 'You're under arrest.' Mamma started crying, but Papà just laughed. He kissed her and told her not to worry as he'd be back later, but PC Williams shook his head. 'I'm sorry, Mr Merelli, you won't. You'll be taken to the army barracks and interned indefinitely.'

'A prisoner of war,' the army officer added.

'But I live here for years now,' said Papà. 'I open this cafe, I work here and have friends. Mussolini is a clown. My sister and her husband, Mario, come away from Italy to be here in Wales too!'

'I've got orders,' the army officer said. 'I'm giving you

and your brother-in-law five minutes to get what you need and come with us.'

I realised that what was happening was not going to be sorted in a few days. 'I'm going with Papà,' I said.

'No. You're under age,' said the army officer. 'And you were born here, which makes you British.'

'I'm Italian!' I shouted.

'Listen!' Papà said as he grabbed me by the shoulders. 'You're in charge now. You have to help Mamma and Zia. I need you to be brave and run the cafe like you know how. One day the war will be over and everything will be back to normal.'

He kissed me and said goodbye to Mamma, then he and Mario were taken away. I couldn't understand how it could have happened. Why did the British think they needed to put all the Italians under guard? They did the same with Germans all over Britain, of course. At that moment, with all the confusion and anger in my head, I still had to open the cafe. Mamma wanted to close it. 'And live on what?' I said.

It was all that was left to us. It was all we had. So we opened."

Joe stopped the tape. He sat there in amazement – he'd had no idea this had taken place. He went straight downstairs.

TWENTY THREE

Gwen was the only customer as Joe entered the cafe. Mimi was sitting with her. "Mam," said Joe. "Did you know that Great-Granddad was arrested in the war?"

"Yes, it was terrible," she said. "Some of the Italians had been living in Wales for years, even longer than him, but it made no odds. They weren't fascists, but the government decided to intern them just in case."

"But why?" said Joe. "What were they afraid the Italians would do?"

"They thought that if they had sympathies towards the fascists they'd disrupt the war effort over here," said Mam. "But Nonno's papà didn't agree with what Mussolini was doing, or Hitler, obviously. What brought this up?"

"I was listening to the tapes Nonno's recorded," said Joe.

"Oh," she said and breathed in deeply.

"You look tired, Mam."

"Yeah. Didn't sleep well last night."

"Why don't you go upstairs for a rest?" Joe said. "I'll take over until closing."

"Thanks, love." She kissed him and went upstairs.

Joe made a cup of tea and took it to Gwen. "On the house," he said as he joined her and Mimi.

"Oh, ta, Joe," said Gwen. "I hear your mam's going to close the cafe?"

"Yeah."

"It's a such a shame," said Gwen. "Where will I go? Especially now you let us know when the bus is due. Very community-minded."

Joe was surprised, as she didn't exactly spend a lot of time in the cafe.

"Gwen," said Mimi. "Can I ask what you do in the evening?"

"Me? Stay in. Watch telly. Why?"

"Do you go out at night?"

"Oh, no. A night out for me is pushing my wheelie

bin to the front gate."

"What about a meal out with your friends?"

"I can't afford it."

Joe received a text message. "Bus to Ponty is coming."

"That's me," said Gwen. "Bye now."

Joe opened the door for her.

"She's lonely," said Mimi, after she'd gone. "That's why she come here."

Joe realised Mimi was right as he watched Gwen make her way to the bus.

"I would like to hear the tapes I hear you talk about, Joe," said Mimi.

"Nonno's tapes?"

"Yes. You mind?"

"No. Course not."

TWENTY FOUR

Joe enjoyed listening to the tapes again, especially sharing them with Mimi sitting beside him. They listened to the rest of the latest one.

"I heard the window smash in the middle of the night. I knew straight away it was on purpose. I couldn't understand why people were hating us. Hating us for being the same people we'd always been – hard-working Italians. We had to get up in the middle of the night and board up the broken window. I found a brick with a note: 'Fascists go home.' *I didn't show it to Mamma – she was upset enough as it was.*

The next morning I made a point of dressing up in a white coat, just like Papà. I wore a shirt and tie and I stuffed newspaper in his hat so that it fitted me. I was stepping into Papà's shoes until he came back. I made up a sign, which I put over the broken window: 'Business as usual. We are NOT fascists, now or ever.'

I saw people stop and read the sign, and then curiosity got the better of them.

'What happened to Vito then?'

'Where have they taken him?'

'Daft, it is.'

I found out that Italians all over Britain had been interned. Some hadn't been arrested, because they'd become British citizens – so they were left in peace.

Papà had left Italy because there was no work and his family were struggling to make ends meet, so he came to Britain. Now he was somewhere under arrest and we were fighting for survival, all over again.

It was difficult to get information, but finally we found out that Papà and Mario had been taken to the barracks in Cardiff, and were under guard – a prison camp, I suppose you could say. It was a ridiculous thing. Crazy.

I decided to ask around for jobs, just to bring in a few extra coppers. I got the cold shoulder most places, but thankfully Mr Lewis the butcher took me on a few mornings a week while Mamma and Zia looked after the cafe.

It was brave of Mr Lewis. He remembered that Papà had given him a lot of business, but, all the same, he was going against the flow.

It was sometime later, while I was making a delivery for him, that Johnny Corbett was waiting for me in a back alley. He stood there grinning.

'How's it going, Adolf?' he asked.

I didn't feel scared this time, what with everything that was happening. I was in no mood to put up with him.

'I see you had a spot of bother with the cafe window?' he said.

'Was it you?' I asked.

'Me? No. But you Eyeties are not welcome – go back to Mussolini.'

'I was born here.'

'Welsh, are you?' He came up to me. 'Say you love Wales and hate Italy then.'

'I love Wales,' I said, 'and I love Italy. We've done nothing wrong.'

'You're a Hitler-loving fascist.'

They would have set upon me, but just at that moment Mrs Jones opened her back door. 'Hello, Johnny,' she said to him. 'How's your mam?'

I could see Johnny was embarrassed. 'Fine, Mrs Jones,' he said.

'Glad to hear it. Think she'll be happy to hear you calling Beppe a fascist?'

He shrugged.

'OK. Let's go then,' she said. 'Let's go and see her now.' She looked at the others. 'And what about you boys? I know all your mams. Tell 'em as well, while we're at it, shall we? With all that's going on in the world right now you should be ashamed of yourselves. Go on. Get away.'

They went with their tails between their legs.

'Thank you, Mrs Jones,' I said, just managing to hold back my tears. She asked after Mamma and wished a speedy return for Papà. She was an angel.

That's all for now, Joe."

The tape ended. Joe looked at Mimi.

"It makes me feel strange," she said.

"How d'you mean?"

"Well, this cafe. Everything that happened, right here."

Joe nodded. "Yeah, I know. This was Nonno's room back then."

He thought about the history within the walls, like the past was right in front of him. "I wonder who

Mrs Jones was," he said, gazing into Mimi's dark eyes. "She must be someone's mam or gran, mustn't she? Like Nonno is my mam's dad."

"You can find out, Joe," said Mimi.

"How?"

"By asking Nonno."

TWENTY FIVE

The wind was icy.

Joe was self-conscious of his stomach pushing out his rugby top, and he thought that being made to stand in the muddy field was cruel.

"Is so cold," said Mimi, rubbing her arms.

Joe could only nod, as he feared his teeth would chatter if he spoke. Combi was standing on the touchline next to Mimi, wearing a huge coat and eating a Mars bar. "I reckon I'd be good at rugby," he said. "Low centre of gravity, see."

Joe clenched his jaw and glared at him.

Bonner was doing push-ups and punching out his

breath. Then he stood up and grinned at Mimi.

"Aren't you cold?" she asked.

"Don't feel it," said Bonner. He tapped his head. "I blank it out."

Joe wished he could blank out the whole experience.

"Right!" shouted Mr Carter, the coach. "Let's warm up with a sprint to the coloured bollards and back."

As Joe ran he could feel the freezing air cut into his lungs.

"And again!" shouted Carter.

Joe was still running back as everyone else charged towards him on the second lap. He was so out of breath when he came to a halt that he couldn't even return Mimi's sympathetic smile.

"Y'all right, Joe?" asked Mr Carter.

He nodded.

"We're going to do some scrum practice now," he said. "I wanna try you in the front row."

Joe was more concerned with Bonner talking to Mimi on the sidelines. "Go on," he was saying with his arms akimbo. "Feel my stomach – it's like a brick wall."

"I'm sure," said Mimi. "Joe! You OK?"

"Yeah," Joe said, still panting.

"You don't look it," said Combi, pushing the end of the Mars bar into his mouth.

Mr Carter called them together for the scrum and Joe joined the other players in the front row. They stood in a line and wrapped their arms around each other's shoulders; then they bent over, facing the opposing players.

"Lock your feet," said Carter. "Make 'em like steel girders. Then when I say 'set', push like your butt is on fire."

Joe could feel the shoulders of the players behind him against his bottom. He had a sense that something bad was about to happen.

"Crouch ... Bind ... SET!"

They rammed forward and there was a crunch. It felt as if Joe had fallen from a high building and hit the ground head first. He was wedged between the heads of the opposing players. There were growls and grunts, and Joe whimpered as he stared at the muddy ground below him.

The pressure, front and back, was unbearable. It was grinding and relentless, like he was being crushed between two elephants.

When the scrum collapsed, Joe's head slapped on to the ground, pressing into the mud. Bodies fell on top of him. His arms were still locked around the players either side of him, and he couldn't breathe.

I'm going to die, he thought.

He imagined Mimi at his funeral, dressed in black and looking beautiful, Mam and Dad crying, and Combi eating a currant bun. Then he saw Mimi as a beautiful bride, and he felt warm and tingly. Someone took her hand and slipped a ring along her finger.

It was Bonner.

Oh, no.

Joe heard a crash of cymbals and a roll of drums. He saw a huge velvet and gold curtain close before him, like at the end of an opera – then everything went black.

TWENTY SIX

When Joe opened his eyes Mam and Dad were looking at him from the end of the bed. *They look serious*, he thought. *I must be in a bad way.*

He lifted his arm.

"What d'you want, love?" asked Mam.

"Wanted to see if ... if my arm still worked," Joe whispered.

"All your body works, Joe. You blacked out – no harm done."

"No harm done!" he said. "Crushed to death, I was."

"I'm sorry, Joe," said Mam. "Perhaps rugby was the

wrong thing to try."

Joe wondered what the "right" thing would be, but decided not to ask. "How many days have I been here?"

"Days?" said Mam. "Joe. You were out for a few seconds, and they took you straight to A&E. You'll be fine."

"When we picked you up," said Dad, "you were muttering something about Bonner's wedding."

"That's right," said Mam. "What was that all about?"

"How's Mimi?" Joe asked to avoid the question.

"She's fine," said Mam. "She wasn't in the scrum, Joe."

"I meant, how is she after the shock?"

"What shock?"

Joe saw a look pass between them. "The shock of seeing me crushed to death," he said.

"She was devastated, Joe," said Mam. "Pacing up and down and wringing her hands, she was. It was like an opera. She's downstairs now, cooking you a special soup."

"Special soup?"

"Yeah, for people who've had near-death experiences."

"Oh, there's nice of her."

"She went to see Nonno too," said Dad. "And he gave her another tape." He nodded towards the cassette player on the desk.

"Oh, good," said Joe. "You should listen to them, Mam."

"I know the story," she said. "Oh, and there's news – Mr Malewski's made us an offer on the cafe."

"Mr Malewski?"

"Apparently he wants to turn it into a restaurant."

"Restaurant! But I've got ideas, Mam," said Joe.

"I've got a few myself," she said, "but I'd be arrested. Look, I haven't accepted the offer – people round here won't thank me for helping them take over the town, but it's an offer."

There was a knock at the door and Mimi entered with a tray.

Joe smiled to see her. She seemed even more beautiful somehow – *glowing*, he thought. Then he saw Combi follow her in. "All right, Joe? Brought you Zombie Wrangler."

Joe would have preferred to be alone with Mimi, and he certainly wasn't in the mood to be killing zombies. Combi set up the game console as Mam and Dad left.

Joe tasted the soup. It was lovely. "*Grazie*," he said. "*Stupendo*."

"*Prego*," said Mimi as she sat on the end of the bed.

"Little more basil, maybe," he added.

Mimi glanced at him, and Joe smiled.

"Have you played Zombie Wrangler, Mimi?" Combi asked.

"No. I don't play these games."

Joe rolled his eyes for Mimi's benefit. He gathered his fingers and shook his hand, but Combi was already handing her the controller. "I've set it on 'easy'."

The screams, zaps and noise of the game didn't help Joe's head, which was still throbbing.

"Ah, you killed me!" said Combi.

"I wish," Joe muttered. He glanced at the tape recorder and decided to put on headphones to listen to the tape.

The annoying noises of the game were replaced with Nonno's soft, close voice.

"I worked extra hard after Papà and Mario were taken away. One day a young man came into the cafe. He asked to speak with us in private. He was the son of one of our Italian neighbours, Domenico Zecchini. Well, this boy, Lou Zecchini, was born in Wales like me, and he'd been called up for the war. He was one

of the soldiers at the barracks in Cardiff, guarding the interned Italians.

'It's crazy, this internment,' Lou said. 'My dad was arrested and interned at the barracks, so now I'm guarding him – my own dad! It's insane. But I'm not allowed to speak out as I'm in the army.'

He banged the table with his fists, he was so angry.

He'd brought us a message from Papà and Mario. They were being treated well and were going to be moved soon, but they didn't know where.

Lou took a big risk getting that message to us.

'What if I were to come to Cardiff?' I asked. 'D'you think I could see Papà?'

Lou shook his head. 'No visitors allowed.' Then he had a thought. 'There's a far side of the camp, away from the road. The men are allowed outside between eleven and twelve. You can talk through the wire fence. I'll let them know the day you're around, but if any of the guards spot you they'll send you packing.'

That night me, Mamma and Zia prepared food and some wine in the hope I could pass it to them. Me and Mamma wrote a letter to Papà, and Zia wrote one to Mario.

The next day I arrived at Cardiff station and walked to the army barracks, which were a few miles away. I had the food in a duffle bag. I also had a pair of pliers in my pocket, which was a bit silly, but if Papà wanted to escape then I wanted to help him.

When I got to the barracks I checked my watch – I was early. I could see the guards at the gates but I couldn't see Lou. So I walked round to the far side and waited behind a tree. I was shaking with nerves. There was a platoon of soldiers on drill with a sergeant shouting orders at them. I can still hear the crunch-crunch of their boots on the tarmac.

At eleven o'clock on the dot I saw men being led out into the courtyard. They wandered around, under guard. I saw Papà and Mario straight away, just by the way Papà walked with his hands behind his back, as if he was taking a *passeggiata*. Lou must have spoken to them because they were looking for me. I went up to the fence. Of course, I didn't want to be spotted so I just raised one arm and hoped they'd see me. They did, and slowly came towards me. I did my best to hold back my tears as I knew that we might not have much time. I forced a smile as they came to the fence.

'Ciao, *Papà*.'

'Ciao, *Beppe*.'

I passed food through the fence, but the salami and the wine were too big.

'How is Mamma?' Papà asked.

'She's OK, but no one tells us anything.'

He nodded. *'They're moving us.'*

'Where to?'

'Liverpool. They are sending us away, on a ship.'

I tried to speak, but Papà flashed his eyes wide. 'Listen! They are sending us both to Canada. You'll have to look after everything, Beppe. You're in charge.'

'But why Canada?'

'They think we are enemy aliens, and in Canada we'll be far away. I'll be back, Beppe. I promise.'

I passed the letters from Mamma and Zia through to him and Mario, and then I heard a shout. A soldier was running towards us. Papà put his fingers through the fence. I clasped them and started to cry.

'Get away from this fence!' the soldier said.

'I'm talking to my son!' Papà's voice was hard and dark, and it made the soldier step back. 'Don't be afraid,' Papà said to me. 'One day we'll laugh about this.' He smiled, but it wasn't his usual smile. He seemed scared, and I'd never seen him scared before. I remembered the salami and the wine, and pleaded with the soldier. 'Will you take these for them? Please?'

He checked around. 'Throw them over and go quickly.'

I threw the salami and wine over the fence, which got the attention of the other Italians. 'Go,' said Papà. 'Go back to the cafe. Bacio per Mamma.*'*

Walking away from that fence was the most painful thing I've ever done in my life. I couldn't believe that everything had turned so bad in such a short period of time. I hated the British and I hated the Italians for joining Hitler. I've never felt so angry, or so scared, and I wondered if I'd ever see Papà again.

I'll stop for now, Joe."

It all seemed to be getting worse for Nonno, and sending Italians to Canada was mad. Joe realised that Nonno was running the cafe when he was no older than he was. He was feeling peculiar – sort of tingly and a little scared. He thought about what Nonno had said about everything turning bad so quickly.

"Time is precious," he said aloud.

Mimi turned away from the video game and smiled.

"Fifty-seven zombies I killed, Joe," said Combi. "You wanna game?"

Joe got up and went to the bedroom window.

"You OK?" asked Mimi.

"I'm fine." Joe gazed down at Mr Malewski's Emporium. The cafe might be sold to a man who would turn it into a restaurant, and take it away from Joe's family forever. "It's up to me now."

TWENTY SEVEN

Joe sneaked out without telling anyone. He hadn't a clue what he'd say to Mr Malewski but he wanted to go all the same.

The shop was busy and Joe wished he'd asked Mimi to come with him. He wandered down the aisle, looking at the produce. "You liked the sausage, Joe?" asked Marta. "Why not try a different one?"

"No, thanks," he said. "Why does your dad want to buy my cafe?"

"To start a restaurant. Good business," she said. "Maybe one day I'll own your cafe, as well as Emporium." She laughed, which Joe thought she did a bit too often.

Mr Malewski walked up to them, together with Dariusz, who was carrying a leg of ham over his shoulder. Joe felt like he was surrounded. "Why don't you buy one of the other shops for your restaurant?"

"No kitchen," said Dariusz. "You have kitchen, tables and chairs – a restaurant. Job done. Where is Mimi?"

"Around," Joe said.

"She has boyfriend?" Dariusz asked, staring at him with his fierce blue eyes.

Joe was irritated by the question. He pulled the corners of his mouth down and shrugged at the same time. It worked and felt natural.

"Did your mother take my offer yet, Joe?" Mr Malewski asked.

"Don't buy the cafe, please," he said.

Mr Malewski frowned. "Why?"

"People don't eat out any more. Not around here," said Joe, using Mam's own argument.

"Disagree," said Mr Malewski. "When people are away from home they come together. We will cook food for Polish, Russians, et cetera, et cetera. Good business."

"Good business," repeated Marta.

Through the shop window Joe saw the cafe across

the road. It was closed and seemed all too sad. He imagined it brightly lit, full of people eating and raising their glasses. "Why don't you do a trial?" he said.

"Trial?"

"Use the cafe one evening. Cook meals for the Polish or whoever and ... you pay us for using the cafe."

Mr Malewski glanced at Dariusz, then back at Joe. "No."

"Wait, wait," said Marta. "It's a good idea – try before we buy!"

Mr Malewski spoke to Dariusz in Polish. Dariusz shook his head. Marta spoke to them both, flapping her hands to get their attention. She turned to Joe. "How much do you want for one night using your cafe?"

Joe didn't have a clue, but found himself saying, "Fifty per cent of profits."

It was odd – he had spoken so confidently.

"Fifty per cent! Too much," said Mr Malewski.

"OK. Sixty–forty to you," said Joe.

"Sixty–five, thirty–five," he replied.

Joe did the hand gesture under Mr Malewski's nose. "If you buy the cafe you'll have to spend a lot of money," he said. "This way you don't lose."

"And I help cook."

Joe turned and saw Mimi.

"OK," said Mr Malewski. He spat on his hand and held it out.

Gross, thought Joe, but he shook on the deal, and Marta clapped.

"You're not serious?" said Mam, standing in the lounge with Dad.

"Is great idea," said Mimi.

Joe did the gesture with his hand. "We can't lose. Mr Malewski and his son provide the food and cook it, and we get forty per cent of the profits."

Mam was staring at his hand. "How do we know he'll give us forty per cent?"

"We make sure," said Mimi. "We find how much he charge and how many come to eat." She pulled at the skin under her eye with a finger. "I watch them."

"You should have consulted me, Joe," said Mam.

"Sorry," he said. "But can't we just give it a try? Please!" He did the hand gesture again. "It's free money."

Mam felt his forehead. "How you feeling, Joe?"

"Never better," he said.

TWENTY EIGHT

The next day Joe went to see Nonno at the hospital and explain about Malewski's evening meals in the cafe.

"Sixty–forty, you say?" Nonno asked.

"Yes," said Joe.

"How many nights?"

"One so far – Polish night ... for people from Poland."

"And what did your mam think?"

"Not exactly 'appy," said Joe. "But if it works out then Mr Malewski might not need to buy the cafe, will he? He can just use it in the evenings."

"Maybe," said Nonno. "How you feeling?"

"Fine... I been wanting to ask you," said Joe. "Who was Mrs Jones? You know, the one that saved you from Johnny Corbett in the back alley?"

Nonno's half-smile was bigger, as if the muscles in his face were getting stronger. "She was lovely, Joe. She had a lovely daughter too – Gwen."

"Our Gwen?"

"Yes."

"Does she know that her mam saved you that time?"

"She wasn't even born, Joe."

"Still. Be nice to tell her."

Nonno began to eat the food and Joe was struck by a thought. "Who taught you to cook, Nonno?"

"Papà and Mamma."

"Mam doesn't cook much, does she?" said Joe.

"No."

"Why?"

"She always let me do it," said Nonno. "I like to cook."

"I was telling Mimi about your lasagne," said Joe. "I wanna cook it sometime."

"You like Mimi, don't you?" said Nonno.

Joe wished he could stop the blood racing to his cheeks.

* * *

When Joe got back to the cafe there were boys lined up against the window. They were cupping their hands over their eyes to see inside.

As he entered, Mam said, "Can you have a word with your schoolmates, Joe? They're gawping and drooling on the window – it's putting the customers off, and they're not after a hot drink either, if you follow my drift."

Mimi entered the cafe from the kitchen. "Hello, Joe."

The cafe doorbell clanged with the surge of boys entering and shouting orders for drinks. Combi pushed his way to the front. "All right, Mimi?"

"Now, boys!" shouted Mam. "One at a time, please."

Joe tried to push them back, like a rugby forward.

"Get back, you RABBLE!" shouted Bonner, standing in the doorway.

The boys fell silent and backed away.

"Thanks, Bonner," said Joe.

"Still alive, I see?" said Bonner, slapping Joe on the shoulder. "Not built for rugby. You need a body like mine, see."

He walked up to Mimi. "*Prynhawn da, ferch brydferth.*"

"What language is this?" asked Mimi.

"Welsh," said Bonner. "Means 'Good afternoon, beautiful girl'."

Mimi laughed. "*Grazie.*"

"Come to invite you to dinner," Bonner said. "At my place. Mam's cooking."

Joe panicked, and he felt Combi nudge him in the ribs.

"She can't," said Joe.

Mimi turned to look at him.

"Why?" said Bonner.

"She's ... she's helping Mr Malewski to cook."

"When?"

"Thursday," said Joe.

"I meant tomorrow," said Bonner.

"OK," said Mimi.

Bonner beamed. "Tomorrow it is. Right, boys – Chicken Box. About turn!"

Combi nudged Joe again as the boys followed Bonner out.

"Will you quit nudging me," said Joe.

"Well, you gotta do something," whispered Combi.

"Like what?"

"She's your cousin – you gotta protect her."

Joe had a mind-flash of himself as the heroic tenor in an opera, sword at his side, facing Bonner, who was dressed in black and had a goatee beard.

"I'll follow him to the Chicken Box," said Combi. "See what I can find out."

"You do that," said Joe. "Enjoy the greasy food."

"Jealous," said Combi as he walked out.

TWENTY NINE

Joe sat with Mimi to listen to the new tape from Nonno.

"Do you really want to go to Bonner's for dinner?" he asked.

"Yes. I like to try different food and cooking, Joe."

"Want me to go with you?"

"No. Is OK."

Joe imagined Mimi and Bonner at a candlelit dinner table. His stomach grumbled; then he was calmed by the sound of Nonno's voice.

"The day we heard, I was behind the counter as usual,

with Mamma and Zia. It was the third of July nineteen forty. Lou rushed into the cafe, his eyes looking wild. 'Did you hear?'

'What?' Mamma asked him.

'The ship was sunk.'

'What ship?'

'The ship that was taking the Italians to Canada. Hit by a torpedo.'

Mamma started crying.

'We don't know Papà was on it,' I said. 'We don't know anything.'

Lou shook his head. 'There was only one boat taking interns anywhere – the Arandora Star.'

It turned out he was right. The Arandora Star was sunk by a German submarine as it sailed to Canada from Liverpool. It took a long time to get confirmation, but finally we were told that Papà and Mario were on board. I remembered Papà looking at me through that wire fence at the barracks. I held that picture of him in my head, and I remembered thinking that it would be the last time I saw him. It was only later that we heard there were survivors; but who had survived, and how many, we didn't know.

As the news filtered through, people who had deserted us were coming back to say they were sorry. I was so angry – it seemed as if the Italians could now be forgiven *because of the irony that the ship had been sunk by a German torpedo.*

We had to sit tight and wait to hear if Papà and Mario were dead or alive..."

Joe stopped the tape. He was totally shocked.

"That is awful," said Mimi. "They send them away and then..."

"Sunk. Torpedoed," said Joe. He pressed play to hear the rest.

"One day PC Williams came in with a sack. It was full of money – contributions from people to have the window replaced. I started shouting about the fact that Papà could be dead and that when he was arrested we got little sympathy, only bricks through the window. 'It was guilt money,' I said. Mamma took the money off him, telling him it was a nice gesture.

The next day an army officer came in with PC Williams. They were very serious. I held my breath. They informed us that Papà had been rescued from the sea and taken back to Liverpool, but there was no sign of Mario. Zia broke down, and Mamma did too, but I was so happy. Of course I felt sorry for Zia, but Papà was alive.

'There's something else,' said PC Williams.

'What is it?'

'When your father was brought back to port he was interned again—'

'What? They're still going to intern them – even after this?'

'Beppe, listen to me,' said PC Williams. 'Your father escaped. He's on the run, and he's only making matters difficult for himself. The army are on the lookout for him. If he comes here, my advice is to tell him to give himself up.'

I kept my calm until they'd gone. I was furious but happy at the same time.

'Papà'll show them,' I said. 'What's the point of giving himself up? So they can put him back on another boat to Canada, and be torpedoed again? He did the right thing, Mamma.'

I wanted to see him again, but at the same time I wanted him to keep safe and away from Bryn Mawr."

Joe could feel Nonno's happiness, as if it was great news that had just happened. He went downstairs with Mimi to see Mam.

"Did you know about the *Arandora Star* sinking?" he asked.

"Of course I did."

"Why didn't you tell me?"

"Nonno didn't like to talk about it really. Anyway, your great-granddad survived, Joe – unlike poor Mario, who drowned."

"Is strange," said Mimi. "If Mario had not died, I would not exist."

"How?"

"Think about it, Joe," said Mam. "Mimi's great-grandmother, Nonno's aunt, married again years later, and *then* she gave birth to Mimi's grandmother."

"Oh, I see," said Joe. "And if Vito had drowned too, I wouldn't exist ... or you, Mam. Scary."

"Life is very fragile," said Mimi.

"I'm glad Vito didn't drown," said Joe. "And I'm sorry Mario did ... but I'm glad he did too, if you know what I mean."

Mimi smiled.

"I'd better crack on with dinner," said Joe.

"You? Is OK," said Mimi. "I cook."

"I want to," said Joe. "I really want to."

THIRTY

The recipe Joe chose was a simple dish compared to the lasagne he used to watch Nonno make, but it was his first solo effort. He put on an opera CD, and Mimi watched over him as he began frying garlic and anchovies. The fishy smell was very strong.

"We cook it for very little," said Mimi, "and then we add the tomatoes."

"I want to try doing it on my own," he said.

"OK. I only 'elp, Joe."

Mam came in from the cafe. "What are you going to cook?" she asked.

"*Pasta puttanesca*," said Joe. "It means 'tart's

spaghetti'."

Mam's eyebrow arched up.

Joe held up his hands. "It's just a recipe, Mam."

"How's he doing?" she asked Mimi.

"Good," said Mimi. "But a bit bossy."

"Why don't you check on the customers?" Joe said as he guided them into the cafe and closed the door.

He checked the recipe, and added tomatoes, chillies, capers and black olives. He wished Nonno was with him as he stirred the sauce.

When it was time to boil the pasta Joe asked Mimi to help him weigh out the right amount for four people.

"How will I know the pasta's ready?" he asked.

"You try it as it cooks," said Mimi. "If still hard, more time; if too soft you cook too long. *Al dente* – not too hard, not too soft."

Joe tasted a length of pasta. It was still a little hard. When it was just right, they drained it through a colander and Joe began to put portions on to each plate.

"No," said Mimi. "We mix the pasta in the pan with the sauce."

"But the picture in the recipe book has the sauce on top of the pasta," said Joe.

"Is wrong," said Mimi. "We mix. The sauce must

stick to the pasta, for taste. Doesn't matter what it look like – taste is more important."

"All right," said Joe.

They mixed the pasta and the sauce together.

"*Bravissimo*," said Mimi.

Joe glanced at Mam, who was watching from the doorway. When he caught her eye she smiled and said, "Well done."

As they set the table Joe worried that the meal would taste horrible and everyone would go hungry, though he was soon encouraged by Dad. "Smells champion, Joe."

"Yes, thank you," said Mam.

Joe waited anxiously for Mimi to try it. He watched her twirl her fork in the spaghetti and taste it. "Is very good, Joe," she said. "*Buonissimo*."

"Yes, lovely," said Dad and Mam.

When Joe tried it he was pleased. It was fishy, and he liked the comforting heat from the chilli. He felt content watching them eating the food he'd made.

"So, Mimi," said Mam. "When d'you think you'll be going back to Italy?"

Joe felt that the atmosphere of the first meal he'd cooked was ruined.

"Nonno wants her to stay," he said.

"What? When did he say that?" asked Mam.

"Today," said Joe, though it wasn't completely true. "When I went to see him. He said he wanted her to stay because ... while he's in hospital he wants you to have as much help as possible, Mam."

"Well, he never said it to me."

"He's had time to think about it, hasn't he?" said Joe. "Oh, and he prefers Mimi's food to the hospital's. He reckons he'll get better quicker if he eats her food."

Mimi grinned, but Mam was looking at him like she didn't believe him.

"And we need to diversify," Joe added.

"What?"

"I was watching this programme on telly. Apparently the key to business success is diversity, this guy was saying – extending your business activities to disparate areas ... not desperate, disparate. Had to look it up; it means different."

Dad's mouth was hanging open.

Mam put her hand to Joe's forehead. "Len," she said. "Can you take him to Dr Dhital in the morning?"

"I feel fine," said Joe. "I just feel different about the cafe."

"Different how?"

"I was watching another programme on the telly and some guy was selling his granddad's war medal.

He got forty pounds for it." He did the hand gesture. "A paltry forty quid!"

Mam grabbed his fingers. "And so?"

"So what was the point of selling it?" said Joe. "It was his family's history!"

"Yes, but... Oh, I see," said Mam with a sigh. "The cafe's worth far more than forty quid, Joe, and you're going to the doctor's tomorrow so he can check you over."

"I'm fine!"

The phone rang and Dad picked it up.

"Hello... Oh, hello, Gwen... Oh, we can't have that, can we... I'll come round." He hung up. "Gwen's light's gone out in her bathroom – said I'd go round."

"I'll come with you, Dad," said Joe. "I wanna ask Gwen something."

He was glad to get away.

THIRTY ONE

"Oh, I'm a nuisance, aren't I?" Gwen said as she opened the door.

"You are," said Dad. "We were saying what a nuisance you are on the way here. Weren't we, Joe?"

"We were," said Joe, joining in the tease.

Gwen appeared concerned until Joe and Dad burst out laughing.

"You 'ad me going then."

Gwen began chatting as Dad checked over the wiring. "It's amazing what you find out on the Internet at the library," she said. "They're running a scheme, see, where they help you look up your family tree. Well, you'll never guess... My uncle, on my father's side, was a gardener for Aneurin Bevan – the founder of the NHS!"

"Was he really?" said Dad. "Jump the waiting list at the hospital with that info."

"D'you think so?" said Gwen.

Dad laughed. "You never know. Joe! Power on!"

Joe flicked the switch and the light came on. "That seems OK now, Gwen," said Dad. "Loose wire."

"Thank you, Len. Now, how much do I owe you?"

"Don't start."

"Oh, no, c'mon." She turned to Joe. "Tell him to let me pay."

"He won't, Gwen."

Dad started packing away his tools. "Tell you what," he said. "Call it 'undred quid..." There was a glimmer of fear on Gwen's face, then Dad added, "When you win the lottery."

She laughed, and Joe remembered what Mimi had said about her being lonely. "Why don't you come round for dinner, Gwen?"

Gwen's laugh faded. "How d'you mean, Joe?"

"To our home, over the cafe, for dinner one evening."

By the expression on Dad's face Joe was worried he'd put his foot in it, then Dad said, "Yeah... You been a loyal customer, Gwen. We got a proper Italian in, as you know. Lovely grub, Mimi does."

Gwen smiled. "Well, I don't know what to say. I'd love to."

As they drove back Dad said, "That was nice of you, Joe. Inviting her."

"Will *you* tell Mam?" said Joe.

"Oh, I don't think she'll object, but you get any other bright ideas just put 'em past me first, yeah?"

"OK," said Joe. "I was thinking... I never knew you subbed the cafe."

"Well, I don't mind," said Dad. "But listen, Joe, I don't like to see your mam so wound up – like with this business with Malewski."

"I didn't do it to wind her up, Dad. I just don't want the cafe sold."

"I know, Joe. But I remember the cafe when I first started courting your mam. Back then it was still a busy place, but Bryn Mawr is not the same as it was."

"That's what I keep hearing – but it's a town with people, lots of people," said Joe as he shook his hands in exasperation.

"I noticed you're using your hands a lot, Joe," said Dad. "What's this mean?" He held his fingers and thumb together. "It's not rude, is it?"

"No," said Joe. "It's Italian."

"Oh."

"Helps you get your point across, Papà."

Dad glanced at him.

"Papà means dad, Dad."

"I know."

Joe grinned at him.

THIRTY TWO

Joe was excited and nervous as Mimi opened the valve to let the water into the chamber of the espresso machine. She stood with her hands on her hips, waiting. Mam and Dad watched from the doorway. "Switch on, Joe," said Mimi.

Joe flicked the switch on the wall and a small red light came on. "What happens now?" he asked.

"The water heat up. We grind the coffee and fill this." She held up a small container with a handle. "Then we pull the lever down to push hot water through, and the fresh coffee come out into a cup."

Mimi poured coffee beans into the grinder and

switched it on. It made a loud growling, crunching noise.

"Is it broken?" asked Joe.

Mimi shook her head. "Is fine!" she shouted over the din. Joe could smell the freshly ground coffee; it was deep and strong.

It wasn't long before he could see steam rising from the top of the machine. Mimi scooped the ground coffee into the filter, then attached it to the espresso machine. She shifted the handle so that it clicked into place. "Is ready."

She placed a cup under the tap and stepped back. "Pull the handle down, Joe."

Joe reached up to the handle that stood upright on top of the machine and pulled. It was stiff, but as it came down there was a hiss and a gurgle as the water passed through the filter. Dark-brown coffee dribbled out of the tap and into the cup. The smell of coffee was now ten times more powerful, but Joe was disappointed by the amount that came out. "It's not much," he said.

"Because it is espresso, Joe – *very*, very strong," said Mimi. "Now we add milk."

The milk was heated and frothed. There were more noises and lovely smells as Mimi made coffee for Mam and Dad.

"I make one for Joe?" she asked.

"Oh, I dunno," said Mam.

"Please," said Joe.

"OK, but lots of milk, otherwise you'll be up all night."

Joe was given a little sugar in his, and then they tasted the coffee.

"Oh," said Dad. "I'll have one of these in the morning – speed me up."

"It *is* lovely," said Mam. "Not sure the customers will spot the difference."

"Mam, they must do," said Joe. "I can."

"Don't drink it all," she said.

Joe wiped the side of the San Marco with a cloth. "Beautiful though, innit, Mam?"

He saw her nod in the machine's gleaming silver reflection.

THIRTY THREE

Joe remembered that he and Nonno had sat in the same waiting room only a matter of days before, and Nonno had remarked that the cafe had once been as full. The tannoy clicked and Joe heard, "*Mr Khan to Dr Foster, room three.*"

He remembered the last tape he'd listened to, and what Nonno had had to deal with. So much had changed for him back then, and changed for the worse. He breathed deeply and sighed.

"What's the matter, Joe?" asked Dad.

"*Mr Davis to Dr Dhital, room two.*"

Right at the moment Joe heard the announcement

an idea came to him. He gazed around the waiting room.

"Joe?" said Dad. "They just called us."

Dr Dhital shone a torch into Joe's eyes. "Well, you seem fine after your little accident," said the doctor.

"I wouldn't say it was 'little'," said Joe.

The doctor stepped back and looked him up and down. "Perhaps a bit overweight."

Joe thought he had a cheek, especially when the chair creaked as the doctor sat back down. "Any double vision?" he asked.

"No," said Joe.

"Loss of memory?"

"No."

"Headaches?"

"Only when I get asked a lot of questions."

"Don't be rude now," said Dad.

Dr Dhital laughed, and Joe thought it was a good moment to ask, "How come people have to wait so long in the waiting room?"

"Joe!" said Dad.

"I just wanna know the reason."

"Medical attention takes time," said Dr Dhital. "Some people have complicated problems that need time to examine, and what they don't realise is that doctors have to write up notes after they see every patient."

"Bet they moan to you about the wait," said Joe.

"Yes, all the time, but if we rush a decision or a diagnosis it could have very serious consequences."

"It's just that I had this idea, just now," said Joe.

"Idea?"

"The waiting room fills up and people get impatient, right? They forget that you're under a lot of pressure."

The doctor nodded.

"So I thought, what if people could wait in the cafe instead?"

"Now, son..." said Dad.

Joe was on a roll. "They could have refreshments. And when you and the other doctors are ready, you call them through and they make their way over."

"But how?" Dr Dhital asked. "How would they be called through?"

Joe turned to Dad. "You could wire up the tannoy system here to the cafe, couldn't you?" he asked.

"Now, hang on—"

"The cafe is a couple of minutes away from the surgery, if that," said Joe. "And they won't *have* to wait in the cafe. We'll just be giving 'em the choice."

The doctor glanced from Joe to Dad. "I don't know what to say," he said as he picked up the phone.

Dad forced a laugh. "Daft, isn't it? I got to say, Doctor, since Joe's little accident we've noticed that he—"

"Mrs Moore," the doctor said into the phone. "Could you come in here."

A few moments later Mrs Moore, the receptionist, came in and the doctor asked Joe to explain his idea to her. She seemed puzzled when he'd finished.

"You'd have fewer people hassling you," said the doctor.

"True," said Mrs Moore.

"And you could get on with your admin," said Dr Dhital. "You always say it's falling behind."

"Very true."

"The patients could come straight to the cafe," said Joe. "And we could let you know they're waiting. They'll be less grumpy and, as I said, they'd have the choice to wait in the cafe or here."

She looked at the doctor, and the doctor looked at Joe.

THIRTY FOUR

"You're having a laugh!" said Mam.

"Dr Dhital reckoned it was worth a try," Joe said.

"It's a loopy idea."

"That's what I thought," said Dad. "But Dhital said for less grumpy patients he'd give anything a go."

"Is fantastic!" said Mimi, clapping her hands.

"People can wait in the cafe," said Joe. "They can have refreshments, and when the doctors are ready they'll call them through. It's only one minute, thirty-seven seconds up the road – I timed myself. We just need a speaker our end. Right, Dad?"

"Easily done," Dad replied with a nervous glance

at Mam.

"Hang on now," she said. "I don't want a cafe full of ill people coughing and spluttering everywhere. I'll have people waiting for buses and people waiting for the doctors; it'll be—"

"It'll be a full cafe?" said Joe.

"Don't be cheeky," said Mam. "It'll be a transient crowd – a constant flow of people and they won't all spend money."

"Mam, first you complained that the cafe was dead – one or two customers stretching out the afternoon with one cuppa – now you're complaining there'll be too many."

"Now, Joe," said Dad.

"Lennie, didn't you mention to Dhital that Joe had had a funny turn since the rugby incident?"

"Yes, I agree," said Joe, shaking his hands in the air. "I *have* had a turn!"

"*And* that he's gone all Italian," said Mam.

Dad nodded.

"I *am* Italian!" said Joe, making the hand gesture.

"There he goes again with the hands!"

Mimi laughed.

"Look, even if we're gonna sell, it won't do no harm, will it?" said Joe.

"Well, I don't see the point, frankly," said Mam.

"It's silly."

Her lips were drawn tight and Joe remembered what Nonno had said about handing her a bad inheritance. "Please, Mam. I've listened to Nonno's tapes, and I just felt... I felt it's worth a try."

She sighed. "When were you thinking of giving it a go?"

"As soon as Dad can run the tannoy cable from the surgery to the cafe," said Joe.

"I might be able to do it tomorrow morning," said Dad.

"And by the afternoon," said Mam, "I'll probably have the bubonic plague."

Joe forced a laugh, but Mam frowned.

THIRTY FIVE

Joe hid behind a wall, breathing hard. He felt bad following Mimi to Bonner's house, but he thought it was his responsibility to watch out for her. He'd left an opera CD playing in his room as a decoy.

When Mimi arrived at the front door Joe positioned himself across the street, behind a van. He shuddered when the door opened and Bonner stood there in a shirt and tie. "Mimi!" he bellowed, as if she was across the street next to Joe. Once she entered and the door was closed Joe didn't know what to do – he hadn't thought that far.

"Joe!"

He turned and saw Combi. "What you doing here?" Joe asked.

Combi tilted his head. "Taking a *passeggiata* ... same as you."

Joe dropped the pretence – he was too concerned about Mimi. "OK. What are we going to do?"

Combi checked around. "C'mon!" he said as he crossed the road.

His confidence made Joe experience a warm tingle of affection. When they reached Bonner's house Combi checked around again, as if his normal occupation was private detective. "Keep guard," he said. "Whistle if someone comes. I'm gonna take a peek."

"Peek at what?" Joe asked.

Combi pointed to the bay window. "There's a gap in the curtain."

Joe watched as Combi crept up the path, crossed on to the lawn and ducked under the window. His head popped up level with the gap.

Joe edged nearer. "What can you see?"

"Bonner's pouring Mimi a drink," Combi whispered.

"Does Mimi look interested or bored?" Joe asked.

Combi held a hand up.

"What is it?"

"Not good," said Combi.

"What?"

"Mimi just laughed."

Joe could feel his anxiety rise, like bile.

"Geez... That wallpaper ... it's giving me a headache," said Combi.

"What now?"

"Bonner's mam just came in with the food. Oh, my God!"

"What?"

Combi turned to Joe. "She's tiny! How could someone the size of Yoda be Bonner's mam?"

Joe pointed to the window. "What's happening now?"

"I tell you what's happening..." a deep voice replied.

Joe turned to see a policeman.

"...You two can explain what you're up to."

When Mam answered the door to the policemen she didn't look pleased.

"Sorry, Officer," she said. "I thought he was in his room."

"Caught him loitering," said the policeman.

"Loitering? He's never loitered before."

"It was Combi's idea," said Joe.

"My apologies, Officer," said Mam. "He's not been

his usual self since he had an accident during rugby training."

"Ah," said the policeman, as if that made it all make sense.

"It won't happen again," Mam said with a glare at Joe. "We'll lock him in the attic from now on."

Joe glanced up at the policeman. "You think she's joking."

Joe paced his room, listening to opera and checking his watch. It was nine thirty and still Mimi had not returned. He looked down from his bedroom window on to the High Street, but saw no sign of her. He crossed to the opposite window to look down into the alley. He saw Mimi enter the backyard. She was alone. Joe breathed out with relief and went on to the landing. He timed it so that he came out of the bathroom just as Mimi came up the stairs. "Hello," he said casually. "D'you have a nice time?"

"Yes," said Mimi.

"How was the meal?"

"Quite nice. It was a Welsh stew – bit heavy."

Joe was determined to dig deeper. "Bonner's ... interesting, isn't he?" he said.

Mimi's expression didn't change, which Joe thought was a good sign.

"He's a very big man," said Mimi.

"Yes. He is a big ... *boy*," said Joe.

Mimi opened her bedroom door.

"Apparently," said Joe, "lots of girls quite fancy him. Bonner, I mean."

"Really?" said Mimi. "You know what?"

"What?" said Joe.

"He let his mamma do *all* the cooking, *and* the washing up." Mimi pulled the corners of her mouth down and shook her head.

"Never," said Joe. "Well, I'm shocked."

"*Buona notte*," Mimi said, and kissed him on both cheeks.

"*Buona notte*," said Joe.

He went back to his room tingling with relief.

THIRTY SIX

Joe was enjoying the opera playing on his iPod as he walked to school.

Combi came alongside him and pulled an earplug out. "What happened last night then?" he asked.

"Mam sent me to my room," said Joe. "By the way, for future reference, I blamed you for us being out. I said you wanted Bonner to return a game he'd borrowed off you, and you needed backup as you wouldn't go on your own."

"That's OK. I told my mam I was on a date with Mimi. And anyway, if you'd done your job properly as lookout..."

"Don't start."

"Did Mimi get in late?"

"No. She's not interested in Bonner anyway," said Joe.

"No. She can't be," said Combi. "Impossible."

They continued up the High Street.

"What you listening to?" asked Combi, who was now eating a slice of pizza that he seemed to have produced from thin air.

Joe offered him an earplug. As soon as Combi heard the music his lip curled up. "It's just someone screaming."

Joe shook his head. "It's opera – Verdi's *Il Trovatore*. See, it all starts with this gypsy woman who throws the wrong baby into the fire..."

"What? You're joking?"

"No. She wants to get back at the Count for killing her mam, see. So she steals one of his two babies and throws it in a fire. Problem is, she throws her *own* baby in, by mistake, not the Count's."

"No way."

"No lie. Then when the two brothers grow up they both fancy the same girl, but *don't* know they're brothers, see..."

Combi's eyes narrowed. "When did this happen then?"

"It didn't, Combi," said Joe. "It's opera. Fantastic though, innit?"

"No," said Combi. He bit into the pizza slice. "Want some?"

"No thanks," said Joe.

"Left over from last night," said Combi. "I love cold pizza – sweet."

Joe licked his lips and an idea tingled in his head. "Sweet pizza."

"Huh?"

"I just thought – pizza but with sweet stuff on top, instead of savoury."

"Never heard of it," said Combi.

"Be nice though – sliced apple and banana, sprinkled with coconut or cinnamon."

Combi's eyes glazed over and his mouth dropped open, showing Joe the mashed up pepperoni and cheese. "Where can you get it?" he asked.

"You can't," said Joe. "You'd have to make it."

"Oh don't do that!"

"What?"

"Describe something nice and then say it doesn't exist."

"It does," said Joe. "You just need to make it." He walked on and stopped in front of the betting shop where Dad was passing a cable over the top. "How's

154

it going, Dad?"

"OK. It should be live for this afternoon's surgery."

"I've done some signs to put up in the doctor's waiting room," said Joe. "Mrs Moore said it was OK. You couldn't put 'em up for me, could you?"

"All right," he said. "I hope this is all going to be worth it, Joe."

"So do I, Dad."

"I don't get it," said Combi.

"What?"

"People wait in the cafe to see the doctor, right?"

"That's right."

"But they'll still be waiting the same time."

"Don't diss my idea, Combi," said Joe. "They'll be in a nicer place and have refreshments to hand. It'll be good for them and good for the cafe. It's a win–win."

Combi shook his head. "They won't get it."

"What are you talking about?" Joe said as he made the hand gesture.

"What's with this?" Combi asked, mimicking the gesture.

"You wouldn't understand," said Joe. "It's Italian."

Combi threw his head back and groaned. Joe walked on ahead.

"Has Mimi asked after me?" said Combi as he

caught up.

"No," said Joe.

"Would you tell me if she did?"

Joe sped up, pretending he didn't hear.

THIRTY SEVEN

At lunchtime Joe went straight to the cafe and was disappointed to find it was fairly empty. "Where is everyone?" he asked Mam.

"What d'you mean by everyone?"

"The patients from the surgery."

"They probably prefer to stay there, Joe."

"Well, is the tannoy working?" he asked, just as he heard, "*Mr Jones to Dr Dhital, room two.*"

"It's been driving me nuts," said Mam.

Joe went behind the counter and picked up the phone. He dialled the doctor's number.

"*Bryn Mawr surgery.*"

"Mrs Moore – it's Joe, at the cafe."

"*Oh, hello, Joe.*"

"Did my dad put up the signs?"

"*He did.*"

"But they're not here, Mrs Moore – the patients, I mean."

"*No. They're here as usual, Joe – I don't think they quite believe it.*"

Joe was determined his idea would work, but as he approached the surgery he began to feel nervous. He spotted Combi eating outside the Chicken Box.

"Where you going?" he asked.

"Doctor's. Come with me."

"I'm eating."

"You'll finish it by the time we get there."

"Want some?" Combi asked.

"No."

"Still on your mam's diet?"

"It's rubbish food, Combi. Just like Mimi told us."

Combi stopped and handed his box of chips to a group of boys.

They pounced on it.

"Vultures with no taste!" said Joe.

The waiting room was packed. Joe gazed around at the miserable faces and had a sinking feeling his idea would be ridiculed in Bryn Mawr forever.

Mrs Moore at the reception desk beckoned him over. "Have a word with them, Joe," she said. "I'd love you to make 'em disappear." She spoke into the microphone. "Can I have your attention, please, for a short announcement from Joe, of Cafe Merelli."

Everyone was looking at him and he froze. Combi elbowed him in the ribs.

"See the signs," said Joe, his voice barely a whisper. "On the wall there..." He pointed at the notices. "Like they say, the doctors' announcements are relayed to Cafe Merelli. It's only a few shops up the High Street, as you know. You can wait there and have a hot drink, or whatever..."

The patients continued staring at Joe as if he was speaking Italian, and his armpits began to tickle. He glanced at the seats that he and Nonno had sat in just days before, looking around at the same dour faces. Combi leaned close. "Incentive, Joe – offer them free drinks. People love stuff for free."

"Mam won't have that."

"D'you want 'em in your cafe or not?"

Joe realised he was right. "As it's our first day," he said. "I mean with this trial waiting-room idea, the teas and coffees are free. You won't have to pay."

There was some mutterings among the patients.

"Now, there's an offer," said Mrs Moore.

"Does that include hot chocolate?" someone asked.

"Yes," said Joe, gaining in confidence. "In fact, we have a variety of hot and cold snacks, and the espresso machine is now working for fresh coffee, cappuccino with frothy milk, teas, and hot chocolate with whipped cream. If you follow me I'll escort you there."

Joe and Combi walked out on to the High Street, but Joe dared not look back. "Are they coming?" he asked Combi.

"Loads," he replied. "I ought to get a free Coke for helping you."

When they reached the cafe Joe entered and smiled at Mam. "They're coming."

"Who are?"

"Doctor's patients, Mam. I ... I promised free refreshments, as it's our first day."

"What? Oh, Joe!" Mam covered her face with her hands.

"Incentive, Mrs Davis," said Combi. "It was my idea."

The doctor's patients entered and shouted out their orders. Joe went behind the counter. He filled the coffee filter, connected it to the espresso machine and pulled the handle down.

"Oh, what's that lovely smell?" a customer asked.

"Coffee," said Joe. "Real Italian coffee."

He heard the customers breathe in. "I'll have one!" someone said.

"Me too."

"Fab-*issimo*!" said Joe as he handed Combi a Coke in the midst of the chaos.

Joe was buzzing, though the coffee he'd had certainly added to his excitement. He used lots of hand gestures as he explained his doctor's patients idea to Nonno at the hospital.

"The cafe was full!" he said. "Like the waiting room."

Nonno chuckled. "Now, why didn't I ever think of that?"

Joe was pleased to see him laugh. "I heard the tape last night, Nonno, about the sinking of the *Arandora Star*. It was terrible, and it made me feel ashamed they did that to Italians who'd done no harm."

Nonno's smile was gone. "It's not the whole story," he said. "There's more to come."

THIRTY EIGHT

"The cafe had to go on as normal. People were talking to us again, and gradually our customers came back. Zia walked around like a ghost. I suppose she'd accepted that Mario had drowned, because too much time had passed. It was horrible. I felt guilty that I was happy Papà was alive somewhere.

One day the army officer came in with PC Williams. They asked if we'd heard from Papà. Mamma grasped my hand under the counter, as a warning to keep calm. 'No, we haven't,' I said.

The officer told us that it was illegal to harbour an enemy alien. He glanced up at the ceiling. 'Mind if I take a look around upstairs?'

'Yes, I do mind,' I said. 'He's not here.'

He nodded at me, then went straight up the stairs anyway.

'Sorry,' said PC Williams.

'So you keep saying,' I said.

Of course, the army officer found no one, so he and PC Williams left.

It was like I was fighting my own war..."

Joe paused the tape. "Fantastic, isn't he?" he said to Mimi.

"Yes," she said. The desk light was reflected in her eyes, and Joe thought it made her look like a beautiful diva in an opera.

"A few weeks later a group of miners came in, straight off the shift and black from head to toe. Dai Gwynn asked if they could use the back room for a meeting. 'Sure,' I said. 'I'll bring you some tea.'

As they went in the back I felt proud, because they were speaking to me like I was the boss, while Papà was away. Mamma was upstairs, and I made up a big pot of tea. We'd baked bread earlier, so I toasted some slices and took it through to them. They were short of men in those days, due to the call-up for the war, so it was extra-tough *times for them.*

When I went back into the cafe Johnny Corbett came in with his pals.

'They caught your dad yet?' he asked with a grin.

When you face a challenge in life you either become stronger or you fade to dust, and I could see that Johnny thought he still had power over me. So maybe it was Dai and the miners treating me like I was the boss that gave me confidence, but I glared at Johnny and said, 'You're not welcome in here, or your pals, so you can get out.'

Johnny smirked. 'And who's going to make me?'

I clenched my fists and marched round the counter. It was like I had the strength of a gladiator as I walked up and grabbed him.

We were locked in a wrestle. I remember feeling my back crash into the counter and then against tables. It was strange, but in the middle of the struggle all I thought about was what the British government had done to the Italians and to Papà. I hated them and I hated Johnny.

I could feel the others boys grabbing at me, but I had an arm around Johnny's neck. With all my weight I brought his head down on a table and I heard him squeal.

The next moment the miners were pulling me off. I was out of breath as I stood looking down at Johnny on the ground, his nose bleeding.

Mamma rushed in. 'Beppe. What's going on?'

'Nothing to worry about, Mamma,' I said. 'I told Johnny he's not welcome in my cafe.' I glared at the other three boys. 'And neither are you, you or you.' I pointed to each one as if I was cursing them. 'Now, get him out and don't come back.'

They took Johnny away, and I went back behind the counter. 'Anything more I can do for you gentlemen?' I asked the miners, like nothing had happened.

'No, thanks, Beppe,' said Dai. 'But if you have any more bother, just let us know.'

'Thank you, Mr Gwynn.'

'We left you something in the back for your trouble,' he said as they went.

As soon as they'd gone, Mamma started having a go at me for what I did to Johnny, and we began arguing.

When we went into the back room we saw one of the miners was still sitting there, drinking tea. Me and Mamma stopped dead. The miner's face was all covered in coal dust, but even so, we knew – it was Papà. He was back."

Joe and Mimi sat in silence for a few seconds.

"Nonno's dad smuggled back into the cafe by the miners, and under the nose of the police and the army," said Joe. "Brilliant!"

"Yes," said Mimi, then she took his hand and gazed into his eyes. "This cafe is important, Joe."

Heat ran up his arm. "I know."

"Don't give up."

"I won't."

Joe's hand was getting hot. "What d'you want, Mimi?" he asked. "I mean ... what do you want to do in the future, like?"

"I want to have a restaurant one day, and cook for people," she said. "Is fantastic thing to do."

"Yes," said Joe, even though he'd only done it once.

"Food bring people together," said Mimi. "Is no like when people watch football or go to church... Food bring together family and friends to eat, and talk. And when you cook for people it show that you love them. Good food give enjoyment and make people happy. Is very special... Food is life."

Joe was awe-struck. "Yeah," he said. A peculiar feeling came over him, as if his great-grandfather, Vito, was listening. "You could cook here, Mimi," he said. "Like Mr Malewski's going to do, but you could cook for everyone."

She smiled. "Yes, Joe."

"Your first restaurant," he said.

She laughed and stroked his face.

"You'd be helping us, Mimi," said Joe. "With my plan."

"What plan?"

THIRTY NINE

Joe was worried Mam was going to blow her top as she stood in the kitchen, looking at him and Mimi. "You can't expect us to buy in food and cook lunches on the off-chance we can get the customers."

"Nonno said he'd cover the cost of the food," said Joe. "He wants us to give it a go, Mam, and now we've *got* more customers, haven't we?"

"Captives, more like," said Mam. "I warn you, Joe, I'll check this with Nonno."

"We can cook good food," said Mimi. "Healthy, tasty and clean."

Joe turned to Dad. "You like Mimi's food, don't

you?"

Dad glanced at Mam just as the doorbell rang. "That'll be Gwen, for dinner," he said. "Let's have a nice family meal, yeah?"

Joe opened the back door. "Hi, Gwen."

Gwen had done her hair and put on make-up. "Not usually out this late," she said.

Mam greeted her warmly as she entered.

"My contribution for the meal," Gwen said as she handed over a bottle of wine. "Ooh, something smells lovely."

Mimi nodded and smiled. "*Pasta al pesto.*"

"It's freshly made *pesto* sauce," said Joe. "Quite simple, really – chopped basil, oil and pine nuts with Parmesan and Pecorino cheeses."

The doorbell rang again.

"Who can that be?" asked Mam.

"Probably Vaughan," said Joe.

"Vaughan!"

"Yes, Mam," he said. "Didn't I mention that I'd invited him as well?"

"No, you didn't."

Vaughan entered holding a bunch of flowers and carrying a canvas bag. His hair was gelled into a quiff. He was wearing a suit, with a shirt and tie. He greeted everyone and handed the flowers to Mimi.

"For you," he said.

"Oh, thank you."

Vaughan held up the bag. "And the last of my Brussels," he said, handing them to Mam.

"Flattered," she said.

As the food was served Joe put on an opera CD.

"*Buon appetito*," said Mimi.

They began to eat.

"Oh, this is gorgeous," said Gwen.

"It's like music in my mouth," said Vaughan.

Mimi laughed.

After Joe tried some, he said, "Bit more pepper, I think."

Mimi glanced at him.

"What's the music?" asked Gwen.

"Yeah, it's a bit heavy, Joe," said Mam.

"It's Puccini's *Tosca*," said Joe. "And this is Scarpia singing – he's well nasty."

"Who's he?" asked Vaughan.

"The villain," said Joe. "See, unless Scarpia gets his way with Tosca he says he'll have her boyfriend shot by firing squad."

"Oh dear," said Gwen.

Joe nodded. "Then he promises to use blank bullets, see, and Tosca believes him." The crescendo of chorus and orchestra was building. "But you find out it was all lies, and her boyfriend's shot with real bullets after all!"

Joe stood up, his eyes wide. "Then Tosca sees him, dead and riddled with bullet holes. She runs to the top of the castle. 'Scarpia!' she sings. 'I'll see you before God!' And she jumps. Splat! The end." He shut his eyes as the music thundered to a close.

When Joe looked they were all gazing at him in silence. Vaughan's mouth was hanging open.

"Joe, you been on the coffee again?" asked Mam.

"No."

"Sounds good," said Vaughan. "Wonder if they made a film of it?"

"Well, I'm getting indigestion," said Mam. "Put on some Mantovani?"

Joe and Dad cleared the plates, and dessert was brought to the table in tall glass cups. "*Zabaglione*," said Mimi. "Beaten egg with Marsala wine."

"Oh, my word," said Gwen as she tried it. "I can honestly say, now, I haven't tasted something so lovely in... Well, I haven't – simple as."

Joe was stunned by the taste. It was sweet and creamy, with a warm-tasting liquor.

Vaughan cleared his throat. "They say the way to a man's heart is through his stomach." Joe noticed he was staring at Mimi. "And this food ... is like an express train to my heart."

"D'you mean it's clogging up your arteries?" asked Dad.

"No. No, I mean... Oh, it doesn't matter."

Joe watched them eating the lovely food and realised more than ever that he wanted to cook.

"Well, I just want to say how kind it was of you to invite me," said Gwen. "Touched, I am."

"Hear, hear," said Vaughan.

"Especially to you, Lucia," said Gwen.

Mam seemed surprised. "Me?"

"Yes," said Gwen. "Ever since my husband died, and with my daughter all the way across the world in Australia, the cafe is the one place I really feel welcome. And I know times are hard for this family, *and* this cafe..." She raised her glass. "But I want to wish you all the good fortune in the world."

Mam glanced at Joe as they all touched glasses.

Joe walked to the bus stop with Gwen and Vaughan.

"Did either of you know Lou Zecchini?" Joe asked.

"I did," said Gwen. "He's dead now. His daughter lives in Llanelli, I think. Why?"

"Oh, just an idea I had. There's the bus."

As the bus approached, Joe said, "So are you two up for tomorrow then?"

"Are you sure?" said Vaughan.

"You'll be doing us a favour, honest," said Joe. "Just come after twelve thirty, order a lunch and eat in the cafe. That's all you have to do."

"And it's free?" said Gwen.

"Yes, just for you two," said Joe. "Secret though."

"Exciting," said Gwen.

They saw her safely on the bus and watched it depart.

"Well, thanks again, Joe," said Vaughan. "I don't mind paying for the lunch."

"No," he replied. "I insist."

"Well, I don't get it, but I'll see you tomorrow."

Vaughan turned to go, then hesitated. "Don't mind me asking you, Joe, but is Mimi seeing someone?"

"No, she isn't, but..."

"Yeah?"

Joe pulled the corners of his mouth down to try and make himself more serious. "Now, don't take this the wrong way..." he said, realising his voice came out rather deep.

"No, go ahead," said Vaughan. "Man to man."

"Well, as she's my cousin," said Joe, still with his deep voice. "I gotta look out for her, see ... and the thing is..."

"I've no prospects to offer her," said Vaughan.

"That's it, isn't it?"

"Well..."

Vaughan sighed. "No, you're right... Nearly thirty, no job, and all I've got to my name is a rack of DVDs and an allotment."

"And you live with your mam," Joe added, and immediately felt bad when he saw Vaughan's reaction.

"You didn't mention that to Mimi, did you?" he asked.

"No."

"Good."

Joe placed a hand on his shoulder. "Mimi was saying she was impressed with your allotment though."

"Did she?"

"Yeah."

Vaughan brightened up. "D'you think she'd like me to bring her some parsnips?"

"Yeah, I think she would," said Joe.

Vaughan looked up at the sky. "Check out the moon, Joe. Beautiful, isn't it?"

"It is."

"Night, Joe."

"Night, Vaughan."

Joe watched him go and then gazed at the High Street in the moonlight.

A beautiful street, he thought. *With a beautiful cafe.*

FORTY

A tingle ran up Joe's spine when he saw that people were waiting on the pavement outside the cafe.

"Well, this is a first," said Mam as she opened up.

They came in, and while Mam took the orders Joe asked the names of those waiting for the doctor. Then he phoned through to the surgery.

"Morning, Mrs Moore," he said. "I've got patients here waiting to be called through – there's Mr James, Mrs Patel, Mrs Petrovich with her boy, Ivan..." Joe dropped his voice to a whisper. "I got to warn you his face is swelled up like a beach ball... Then there's Mr Lewis, Mrs Evora and Mr Conway. That's all so far."

"Thank you, Joe. The waiting room is empty here – lovely," she said. *"Only a few repeat prescriptions to do."*

Mr James raised his hand. "We're not obliged to purchase anything, are we?"

"No. Not at all, Mr James," said Joe.

"Told you," muttered Mam. "The last of the big spenders."

"Can I have a tea, please," said Mrs Evora.

"And I'd like a herbal tea, please, Joe," said Mrs Patel.

"Peppermint?"

She nodded and rubbed her stomach. "Not been right for days."

"Coming up."

Mr Conway sniffed the air. "Lovely smell of coffee."

"It's fresh," said Joe.

"I'll take one," said Mr Conway. "Test my ticker."

"Oh, go on. Me too," said Mr James.

"Right you are," said Joe with a satisfied grin at Mam.

"Mrs Evora to Dr Dhital, room two, please."

"Oh, but I haven't had my tea," said Mrs Evora.

"Tell you what," said Joe. "You can take it with you or come back after your appointment and have another, free of charge."

Mrs Evora's face lit up. "Thank you, Joe. I'll be back."

"Giving it away now," said Mam.

"No. Building community relations, actually," said Joe. "And now I'm going to put out the menus for lunch."

He went round the cafe placing on the tables the menus he'd designed on his computer.

"This is our lunchtime menu for today," he said to the customers. "Specially prepared by our relative from Italy – proper Italian cooking. Serving from twelve thirty onwards." There were mutterings among the customers, just as Vaughan came in.

"Morning, all."

"Morning, Vaughan," said Joe. "Usual?"

"Espresso, please – made a new man of me, it has. Mimi around?"

Mimi came to the doorway of the kitchen. "Oh, hello, Vaughan."

"*Buon giorno*, Mimi," he said with a smile. "Brought you some parsnips from my allotment."

"Oh, thank you."

Joe made the coffee and took it to Vaughan, who had settled in a booth. Joe wiped the table, and out of the corner of his mouth whispered, "You still on for later?"

"Aye," said Vaughan. "Looking forward to it. Who wouldn't? A free lunch…"

Joe kicked him under the table. "Sorry," they both said to each other.

"Twelve thirty on the dot," said Vaughan. "Shall we synchronise watches?"

"No need."

Joe checked that Mimi had everything she needed for the lunch serving and then left for school.

On his way a hand slapped on to his shoulder. He winced, knowing who it was.

"How's Mimi?" said Bonner. "Asking after me, was she?"

Joe felt the beginning of acid indigestion, then a thought came to him. "She was, actually."

Bonner stopped. His permanent smile dropped. "She *was*?"

Joe nodded.

"What she say?"

"She goes, 'Bonner's a big man,' and I goes, 'Yes … he is.'"

Bonner stared into the distance. "Big man," he said to himself.

"And she liked your mam," said Joe.

"She liked Mam," Bonner repeated, and Joe saw his eyes well up.

"Mimi's cooking a special lunch in the cafe today," said Joe.

"Is she?"

"Yeah," said Joe. "I tell you, Bon, food is important to us Italians, you know? Really important, and Mimi's well into it."

They walked to school and Joe felt Bonner's arm slip over his shoulder.

"Y'all right, you, Joe."

FORTY ONE

Joe raced back to the cafe at lunchtime. He was nervous as he approached, but when he saw the healthy number of customers in the booths he punched the air. "Yes!"

He entered the cafe and went straight behind the counter. "Hi, Mam," he said. "Taken any lunch orders?"

"No."

The customers chatted over their drinks as they waited.

"Have you noticed," said Joe, "there's a nicer atmosphere in here than in the doctor's waiting room?"

"Can't say I have."

"Look at them, Mam. Chatting, they are. People are nervous waiting to see the doctor – in case it's bad news – but the cafe is a safe place, see. They're happier in here than over there. Deffo."

"*Mrs Shaw to Dr Dhital, room two, please.*"

Joe went through to the kitchen where Mimi was preparing the food. "Smelling lovely, as usual," said Joe. He opened the door and began to waft a large tea towel in the direction of the cafe.

"What you doing?" asked Mam.

"They need to smell before they buy," he whispered.

Mam sighed.

Joe wandered between the tables and adjusted the condiments and menus.

"Mimi!" he called through to the kitchen. "The *minestrone* soup – it's tomatoes, beans, celery, carrots, potatoes, basil and lashings of Parmesan cheese, right?"

"Yes. Right," she shouted back.

A moment later Vaughan entered. He was smiling. "Mmm. What's that lovely smell?" he asked, just as Mam called out, "Bus to Aber arriving!"

Several people got up to leave, pushing past Vaughan.

Joe went up to him and whispered, "D'you think you could go out and come back in – they didn't catch that."

"Oh, OK," he said, and left. Joe went back behind the counter.

"Was that Vaughan who just came in and went straight back out?" Mam asked.

"Didn't notice," said Joe as Vaughan re-entered and walked up to the counter. He winked at Joe.

"Mmm. Something smells nice," he said out loud.

Some of the customers looked up.

"That's the soup of the day, Vaughan," said Joe. "*Minestrone.*"

"Is it *really?*" he said loudly, looking around at the customers. "Well, *I'll* be having some of that, make no mistake."

Joe leaned forward and whispered, "Tone it down a bit, Vaughan."

"Sorry."

"One soup of the day!" Joe called through to the kitchen as Vaughan took a seat.

"What are you up to?" Mam asked.

"Nothing," said Joe.

The doorbell rang as Gwen entered. "Hello, Lucia, Joe."

"Hello, Gwen. Usual, is it?" Mam asked.

Joe thought Gwen seemed nervous. She held tightly to her handbag and glanced at him. "Well, I was going to have my usual," she said. "But ... what's that I can smell?"

"It's the soup of the day, Gwen," said Joe, out loud.

Mam groaned. "I don't believe this."

"*I'm* having it," Vaughan called out.

"Oh, go on," said Gwen. "You only live once."

She took a seat just as Bonner and his gang came in with Combi.

Mimi came out of the kitchen with the bowl of soup for Vaughan.

"Hello, Mimi," said Bonner with an extra-wide grin and a wink.

"Hello," she said as she grated Parmesan cheese on Vaughan's soup.

"What can I do for you?" Joe asked Bonner.

"We come for lunch, haven't we."

"Have you booked?" Joe asked.

"Eh?" said Mam.

Joe gently pressed his foot on to hers.

"Booked?" said Combi.

"Didn't know we had to," said Bonner.

Joe scanned the cafe. "Well, let's see... I can squeeze in you two, but the others will have to wait, I'm afraid."

"That table's empty," said Bonner, pointing.

"It's reserved," Joe said as he came around the counter. "Follow me."

He escorted Bonner and Combi to a shared table and handed them each a menu. On his way back to the counter a customer stopped him. "What's the pasta dish?"

"It's spicy Italian sausage with rigatoni pasta," said Joe. "It's recommended by the chef."

"Thing is," said the customer, "I'm waiting for the doctor to call me through."

"We're serving until half two, sir," said Joe. "I'll reserve a place for you."

He went back behind the counter, and noticed Mam was holding her forehead. "We'll have trading standards on to us!" she muttered.

Joe gave Vaughan a nod, and Vaughan groaned loudly.

The customers turned to look at him. "That's *gorgeous*," he said holding another spoonful of soup to his mouth. "I can feel it doing me good with every mouthful! Vitamins scurrying around my body."

"Could I have a portion?" one customer asked.

"Me too," said another.

"*Mr Collins to Dr Foster, room three.*"

"That's me," said Mr Collins. "But I'll be back and

184

have the pasta."

"Certainly," said Joe. "Two soups!" he called to the kitchen.

"Coming up!" said Mimi.

Joe winked at Mam. "Yeah. Coming up roses!"

FORTY TWO

Joe kept popping to the top of the stairs, curious to look down into the kitchen. Mr Malewski and his son, Dariusz, worked at the cooker, stirring large pots and frying meat. The smells were strong and rustic.

"Strangers in the house," Mam said as she watched TV in the lounge with Dad. "I'm not comfortable."

"D'you want another cushion?" asked Joe.

Mam rolled her eyes. "Don't wind me up, Joe."

"But, Mam," he said. "You might be *selling* the cafe to Mr Malewski."

"Not yet."

Joe went downstairs. He saw Dariusz explaining

to Mimi what they were cooking. She seemed very interested, which made Joe feel jealous. He could hear laughter and chatter coming from the cafe. He glanced inside and saw the customers drinking and talking as they waited for food. It was lovely but he felt left out, so he decided to go outside.

Joe walked along the back alley and out on to the High Street. From the other side of the road he could see the cafe all lit up. People sat in booths chatting, eating and drinking, like it was their last night on earth. He saw Dariusz and Mimi bringing through plates of food and the customers tucking in. It was fantastic. A restaurant, bright and shining in the dark; somewhere to eat good food and be welcomed – "somewhere to be", as Nonno had said. Joe imagined it was what it must have been like when Nonno was his age.

"Hey, Joe!"

He turned and looked up. Marta was leaning out of an upstairs window over Malewski's shop. "Good business, eh?" she said, with a nod towards the cafe. "One day it will be mine."

"You haven't bought it yet," said Joe, feeling irked.

"I wanted to help tonight but Dad said no. Not fair." She pointed at the cafe. "People happy, and eating, and spending money." She chuckled and clapped her hands. "And I hear your lunches are good business too!"

"Not bad," said Joe.

"You should offer international menu," she said. "So you increase your customers. Think about it, Joe... International menu."

Joe shrugged and began to walk back across the road.

"Hey, Joe!" Marta called again.

"What!"

"How old are you?"

"Fourteen. Why?"

She shrugged. "Thought you were older."

Joe was flattered, then he stopped and glanced back.

Marta waved at him and laughed.

FORTY THREE

"Papà sat at the fireside and told us what happened the morning of the sinking.

He was asleep when the explosion woke him. He said he first thought the ship had come into port and crashed into the dock. Mario was sitting bolt upright in his bunk. He seemed to know straight away that they'd been hit by a torpedo. It was quiet, and then they heard shouting and footsteps rushing along the corridor. Papà and Mario joined the crowd making their way up to the deck.

I remember Papà staring into space for a moment, and in a whisper he said, 'I never want to see panic *like that again.'*

Men thinking just for themselves; pushing people aside. On deck people were fighting for a place in a lifeboat. There were men in the water; some were swimming and some were floating on debris, or clinging to each other. The ship was leaning. Time was running out. They knew they'd have to swim.

'There was a man, another Italian,' Papà told us. 'I'll never forget the look of terror on his face. "I can't swim!" he said. "Come with us," I said as I clambered on to the rail, but he wouldn't. Then me and Mario jumped.'

He described the shock of the cold water, and sucking in air as he came to the surface. He looked around and saw Mario, but a second later something fell on him. Someone had jumped from the ship and landed right on top of him, pushing Mario back under the water. The man came up gasping for breath and swam away.

Papà called out, 'Mario! Mario!' He heard metal ripping and groaning and saw the ship lifting out of the sea. He saw the man who couldn't swim, still clinging on to the rail as the ship began to sink. There was a huge eruption of water and the ship disappeared.

Papà never saw Mario again.

He sat there and burst into tears. It was the first time I'd ever seen him cry. Mamma had her arm around him.

Zia was crying. She already knew that her husband had died, but now, at least, she knew how it had happened."

Joe stopped the tape. It was one bad thing after another – the decision to intern Italians, the decision to send them to Canada and the decision by the German submarine to torpedo a ship full of innocent men, including Germans. It was like the plot of an opera, except it was real life. Joe was about to continue the tape when he heard music.

FORTY FOUR

The windows were vibrating.

Joe went downstairs and peered into the cafe. Dariusz was playing an accordion, which was perched on his knee. The customers sang along.

Mimi was clapping in time to the music and laughing. It was the first time Joe had seen her really happy. Mr Malewski and Mr Kempski, the breakfast customer, were arm-in-arm and singing with tears in their eyes.

"Joe!" said Mr Kempski. "I miss my village – just outside Gdansk."

Mam appeared at the doorway. She looked far

from happy. "Mr Malewski!" she shouted, but was drowned out by the music. She turned and went back upstairs.

It was very late when Mam insisted that the customers left.

Joe watched the diners make their way home, singing at the top of their voices. The rain was glistening in the light of the streetlamps, and he was envious that Mr Malewski had cooked for them.

"Was good, eh, Joe?" Mr Malewski said as he wiped down a table. "Polish people work hard, play hard and eat well. We make this town live." He raised his glass. "*Na zdrowie!*"

"Teaching him to drink now, are you, Mr Malewski?" said Mam.

"We celebrate. He's great, your boy," said Mr Malewski, patting Joe on the head.

"Yes he is, but now, if you don't mind, it's very late."

Mr Malewski pulled out a wad of bank notes. "I owe you fifty per cent of money."

"It was forty per cent," said Joe.

Mr Malewski flapped a hand at him. "Fifty, forty. Tonight, I don't care." He counted out the notes on the table. "Good night, Mrs Davis."

Joe put on a CD and opera music played as he

193

helped Mam clear up with Mimi and Dad. He watched Mr Malewski stagger across the road to his shop, singing as he went.

"It was fantastic!" said Mimi. "People eat and sing and are 'appy!"

"Yeah," said Joe.

"I'm not sure it was worth it," said Mam. "I mean, look at the mess in here."

Joe was straightening one of the photos on the wall. "Why d'you hate the cafe so much, Mam?"

He saw the shock in her eyes.

"He's right!" said Mimi to Mam. "I hear Nonno's tapes – this cafe has a heart, but you no care any more."

"I don't think this is any of your business," said Mam.

"Not my business, no, but my great-grandmother come here in nineteen thirty-nine – she 'elp Nonno when his papà was taken away. Nonno ask me to come here. He pay for my ticket. He ask me to 'elp, one last time before is finished, but now I see you give up. *You* don't care..."

"Oh, that's right, I don't care," Mam said, almost smoking with anger. "I've only worked ninety-six thousand hours between these walls – I know because I got a calculator one day and worked it out. From the time I was eighteen – seven days a week, in those days – ninety-six thousand hours and counting." She had tears in her eyes as Madam Butterfly was singing in the background. "And you come along with your cooking and you think you can go back in time and make it like it was – just like that!"

She turned to Joe. "I know what you want, Joe – I get it, but I'm talking about what *I* want." She prodded her chest as the orchestra was crashing to a climax. "My dad earned his rest, but this is me now. My turn. D'you understand?"

"But if you didn't want to work in here why didn't you just say?" Joe said. "Nonno would have understood, but instead you blame these four walls." His heart was going like the timpani in the opera. He pointed to the picture. "This is ours – our family business, Mam. Now I'm listening to Nonno's story, and his Papà's story, and I love it all the more. I don't want it to die."

A tear rolled down his cheek.

"It's late, Joe," said Mam. "I'd like to go to bed." She turned to Mimi. "And you ... you've overstayed your welcome."

Mam went upstairs. Mimi opened the cafe door and went out into the night.

FORTY FIVE

Joe sat on his own and listened to the rest of Nonno's tape.

"Papà had to keep hidden, and for a while he stayed in the attic, but we were always frightened of another visit from the army or the police.

Rationing was going on, and Papà continued to preserve all sorts of food to keep himself busy, but having to stay in the attic every day drove him crazy. I think being held prisoner, even for that short time, had done something to him. So now and again he would dress up as a miner and go out in the evenings. You can imagine how much me and Mamma worried, but he said he needed to get out.

One evening he came back in. 'Come with me, Beppe.' He led me up to the attic. We stood there looking at all the jars of preserved food. 'Use them,' he said. 'People are hungry.'

'But it's for the winter, Papà,' I told him.

'No,' he said. 'People need it now.'

Then we heard Mamma. 'Vito! Beppe!'

When we went downstairs, Dai Gwynn the miner was standing in the back kitchen. 'You need to go, Vito. Someone tipped off the army and they're on their way with the police. Go to my house,' he said. 'You can hide there. My wife will be expecting you.'

Papà and Mamma thanked him, but I was furious.

'Who tipped off the army?'

'We don't know, Beppe.'

'I bet it was PC Williams.'

'It certainly wasn't him,' said Dai.

'How d'you know?'

'Because it was PC Williams who tipped me off to get Vito out.'

I was ashamed of jumping to conclusions. Shortly after Papà left, the army officer arrived with PC Williams to search the place. 'Sorry about this, Beppe,' he said.

'It's a disgrace,' I shouted as the soldiers stomped about

upstairs. Then I whispered to him, 'Thank you.'

What a man, and what a risk he took... There's not much more to tell now, Joe..."

An idea began to form in Joe's mind; he couldn't sleep, so he went downstairs.

He sat in a booth in the darkened cafe. The High Street was empty, and it seemed like a ghost town.

He watched a couple walking across the street. Joe imagined the cafe open and welcoming them inside for a hot drink. They would sit and declare their love.

He smiled to himself as he saw the couple embrace passionately, and he wondered what it was like to be kissed that way.

The lights of the cafe snapped on. "You still in here?" said Dad.

Joe saw the couple pull apart, and in the light he saw it was Mimi and Dariusz. He felt as if his heart had cracked open.

FORTY SIX

Gwen was surprised to see Joe at her house so early the next day. She looked over the list he'd given her.

"Oh, I remember Dai Gwynn," she said. "If that's the same Dai."

"Maybe the library could help?" said Joe.

"Yes. Be a project for me," she said. "I'll ask around too. Lilly Matthews will know some of these, I'll bet."

"Thanks, Gwen," said Joe, then a thought came to him. "Oh, did you ever know a Johnny Corbett?"

"I did. He was the father of Natalie. You know, your mam's friend – the mam of that pal of yours who's always stuffing his face."

Joe's stomach turned, as if he hadn't eaten in days. "Combi?"

"That's right," said Gwen. "What's the matter, Joe? You've gone pale."

"Nothing."

Outside in the street Joe breathed in deeply. His best friend, Combi – the grandson of a bully; a bully who'd picked on Nonno at such a difficult time. He didn't know what to do – suddenly everything was going wrong.

When Joe got back to the cafe he saw that it was busy with customers eating food. Mam was behind the counter. Joe thought she was looking really sad. "'Lo, Mam," he said. "Sorry about last night."

"It's all right," she said. "Listen, Joe, I wanted you to be the first to know... I've decided to accept Mr Malewski's offer."

Joe nodded and gazed around at the customers enjoying their lunches. Vaughan grinned at him as he twirled spaghetti on a fork. "*Buonissimo.*"

"Sorry," said Mam.

Joe could feel that he might cry if he stayed. "It's OK." He decided he couldn't tell Mam his idea right at that moment.

"Oh, and Nonno's coming home," she said.

"When?"

"Few days' time."

"Mam, don't tell him about selling. Not yet."

"It won't be a surprise to him, Joe."

"Maybe, but just not for now."

"OK."

Joe watched Nonno slowly eat the pasta. He wanted to tell him he'd found out that Johnny Corbett's descendant was his best friend, but it was not a nice discovery, especially added to the news that Mam had accepted Mr Malewski's offer, not to mention that Dariusz was Mimi's boyfriend.

"Mam told me you're coming home," he said.

"I'm looking forward to it."

"Me too."

"You listened to the tape, Joe?"

"Yes, and I wanted to hear all about what happened afterwards."

Nonno wiped his mouth. "OK."

"Hang on," said Joe. "I want to tape it."

FORTY SEVEN

Joe was wrapped up in his thoughts as he walked along listening to his iPod.

An earplug was suddenly yanked out. "Listening to opera again?" asked Combi.

Joe glared at him and snatched the earplug back.

"How's my Mimi," Combi asked.

"She's not *your* Mimi."

"'S'up with you?"

"What's up with me is that I know who your granddad was."

"So?"

"Johnny Corbett was nasty."

"I never met him."

This threw Joe for a moment. "Well, he was a bully."

"How d'you know?"

"I know. I've heard it all," said Joe. "Nonno was fighting to keep the cafe going and your granddad was just a thug, making his life miserable."

"What's it got to do with me?" said Combi.

"What's it got to do with you?" Joe glared at him. "Go 'way, Combi, and don't come in the cafe ever again."

He turned and walked away, but the shock and hurt in Combi's eyes stayed with him.

FORTY EIGHT

When Joe got back to the cafe he went up to Nonno's room and put on some opera to take his mind off Combi. There was a knock at the door. "Come in."

Mimi entered and Joe's heart pounded. He stopped the music and pointed at the tapes. "There's more of the story from Nonno."

She came over and sat beside him. "You OK, Joe? I no see you during lunch."

"I was busy... I've had this idea."

"You and your crazy ideas." Mimi smiled at him and took his hand. "Is time for me to leave, Joe."

"No. Don't go," he said.

"I think is better – for everyone."

"Mam's sold the cafe. To Mr Malewski."

"I know," said Mimi. "You see, Joe, I come because Nonno ask me, but I come to 'elp myself too – I can no find work in Italy so I come here."

"But that's OK," said Joe. "That's only what Nonno's dad did."

"Yes, but today a friend call me to say there is a job, in London. In a kitchen. Your mamma sell the cafe so I take the job and go."

Joe couldn't forget the sight of Mimi kissing Mr Malewski's son. "But ... but what about Dariusz?"

"Dariusz?"

"Don't you love him?"

Mimi laughed. "Oh, Joe, Joe. Was only a kiss – I think you say a snog?"

Some snog, thought Joe.

"I like him, sure," said Mimi. "He's hard working ... and I like the stew he cook, but I need to get a job now – I need to work."

Joe glanced out of the window and saw the moon, big and full; its light caught Mimi's hair and he remembered that the tenor in *La Bohème* first sees Mimi in moonlight, when her candle was blown out.

"Did you really like the pasta I cooked the other night?" he asked.

"Yes," said Mimi. She smiled and touched his face. Her hand was cool and soft. "You know, Joe, one day you will make someone very 'appy."

She leaned forward and kissed his cheek.

Joe thought he heard music, like the end of a tragic opera, but realised the CD player wasn't on.

Once he was alone he listened to the last act of *La Bohème*. It began full of joy, with the four students play-fighting, but then Mimi arrived. She was very ill. Rodolfo, who loved her, thought she just needed to rest and she'd be better, but his friends knew she was already dying.

It was too sad, and as the opera ended Joe buried his face in the pillow.

FORTY NINE

Nonno ate the food Joe had brought him while they sat in the hospital ward lounge.

"You're looking loads better, Nonno."

"It's the food, Joe," he said. "So important, good food." He wiped his mouth and took a drink of water. "Your mam said that Combi's mam spoke to her about you and him falling out – what's that all about?"

Joe had a sinking feeling about what Nonno would say. "Not speaking to him."

"Why's that?"

"You'll never guess," said Joe. "I found out he's

Johnny Corbett's grandson."

"I know, and so?"

"You knew? Well, there's bad blood between us now, and I told him so."

Joe saw something in Nonno's eyes he'd never seen before – Nonno was angry, and he was angry at him. "What does it have to do with Combi, or his mother?"

"But he bullied you, Nonno. He tipped over your cart. He was going to beat you up if Gwen's mam hadn't shown up that time. And I reckon it was him who smashed the cafe window."

"I told you the history of the cafe, Joe – my life. I told you about Johnny Corbett because he was part of my life back then. You think I've never behaved badly? Of course I have. I've done things I've regretted…"

Joe tried to speak, but Nonno raised a hand.

"I tell you something about Johnny Corbett that's not on those tapes, Joe. He joined the army, and he fought in the Korean war and in the troubles in Northern Ireland. One day he came into the cafe to say goodbye to me, as he was on a tour of duty. 'We've never spoken about this,' he said to me, 'but I'm ashamed of the way I treated you in the war.' I said the past was the past. We shook hands and I told him to stay safe."

Nonno took a deep breath. "A few months later he was killed in action, and his wife was pregnant with Combi's mam. You did wrong, Joe. I'm disappointed."

Joe tried to speak but his voice was a whisper. "Sorry, Nonno."

"Put it right, and quickly."

FIFTY

It was raining when Joe knocked on Combi's door. His mother, Natalie, opened up. "Oh, it's you. Come to slag off someone else in my family, have you?"

"No, Mrs Morris. I need to see Combi."

"I'm not sure he's interested, Joe," said Natalie. "He was very upset. He's just been zapping zombies since, and the most worrying thing – he's lost his appetite."

"Please," said Joe.

"I'll see if he'll come down."

She went upstairs, and Joe waited nervously. He wanted things back to how they were, but when he

211

saw her come down the stairs he knew they wouldn't be.

"Sorry, Joe," she said. "He doesn't want to see you."

When Joe got to the High Street he stood opposite the closed cafe. It was dark. He tried to imagine it as a Polish restaurant.

"Why d'you look so sad, Joe?" asked Marta, coming out of Malewski's shop.

"Your dad's lucky," he said.

Marta pushed out her lower lip. "Sorry." She held up a vacuum-packed sausage. "You want to try this one?"

"No, thanks."

"Please, Joe," she said. "You try it. If you like it then more people will like our products and the more we sell... Good business, see."

Joe took the sausage just as the lights went out in the shop.

"Oh, what's happened?" said Marta. "Too early to close." She went inside, but Joe noticed all the shops had gone dark. It was eerie, as if the whole town had died.

Marta came out. "Power cut," she said. "Bad for business."

Joe walked round the corner, down the alley

and into the backyard of the cafe. He entered the darkened kitchen. It was quiet, and his sense of unease increased. Perhaps Mimi had already gone. He heard heavy footsteps above, and then Mam charged down the stairs with her coat half hanging off.

"Mam?"

She looked wild. "It's your dad." She ran past him to the back door. "He's been hurt."

FIFTY ONE

Joe gazed down at Dad in the hospital bed hooked up to a monitor. He thought it was ironic that his dad had worked with wires and cables all his life, but now it seemed like the machine was running off him.

"Lennie," said Mam.

Dad opened his eyes and smiled meekly. "Now I know how it feels to get electrocuted," he said. "Professionally embarrassed, I am."

"But you're alive," said Mam, "and that's all that matters."

"I was thinking," said Dad. "What with Nonno in here, and now me, if any more members of our family end up in this hospital people will start talking. So you two be careful, for God's sake."

Joe and Mam started crying.

"Don't go all Italian on me," said Dad, making them cry all the more.

Joe stayed with him while Mam went to tell Nonno and discuss with the nurses what her father would need for his return home.

"I been thinking a lot," said Dad.

"'Bout what?"

"You've got your granddad's spirit, Joe," he said. "I admire it, like I admired Beppe when I first knew him. And I'll tell you something ... something I've never told your mam – when the cafe started getting into trouble because it wasn't making money, part of me was glad."

"Glad?"

"Aye, because I had something to offer, see. I was needed – not that your mam or Beppe ever made me feel unwanted. I suppose it's a bloke thing, from my generation. I had to have purpose. When I sat at the table, back in the early days, I didn't feel like I was contributing. So when customers stayed away and the money in the till got less and less, I felt I was of use."

"That's all I'm trying to do, Dad."

"I know, Joe. Just go easy on your mam."

"I think I'll be glad when it's all over now, Dad, and the cafe's sold off."

"You tried, Joe. No one can criticise you for trying."

Joe suddenly felt deeply tired and hungry.

FIFTY TWO

As Joe and Mam reached the High Street the lights came back on, as if it had come back to life.

"You hungry, Mam?" Joe asked as they entered the kitchen.

"No, thanks," she said. "I'm going upstairs for a rest."

Joe opened the fridge and saw the sausage Marta had given him. He took it out and cut himself a slice. It was smoky and spicy. He liked it, and remembered what she'd said about the more people who liked Polish and other Eastern European products the better for business. "Like Italian food," he said to himself.

After he'd eaten his tea he listened to some opera. He chose Nonno's favourite chorus by Verdi. The music had a strange effect on Joe – as if he was transported to another time and place. The people that were singing seemed sad but determined, and somehow it made him feel more proud of Nonno than ever before. Later, he went upstairs to hear the rest of Nonno's last tape, but when he entered his room he found Mam sitting at the tape recorder. She turned. Her eyes were full of tears. "Mam. What's the matter?"

"I listened to them, Joe. The tapes."

"They're great, aren't they?"

"No."

"No?"

"Oh, of course they are," she said. "I knew the story, but listening to Nonno's voice on those tapes really got to me. I suppose I tried to put it out of my mind, all these years."

Joe sat beside her. "Why?"

"It reminded me of the significance of this house, which made it harder for me to sell – I couldn't erase the past, I wouldn't want to, but I felt I owed it to my dad, my mam and my granddad to keep the place going because of what they went through."

Fresh tears came to her eyes.

"But you *did* run the cafe, Mam," said Joe.

"Aye, and look what happened – it dies a death."

"But you weren't to blame, Mam. Nonno said so himself – people stay at home these days, and the recession and everything."

She shook her head. "Nonno's coming home tomorrow. He's still very ill. Your dad almost died and he can't go back to work – who knows when he'll be able to. It's all on me now."

"And me," said Joe. "We'll be fine, Mam, and we're going to sell it, remember. All we can do is carry on, like Nonno and his mam did back then. We carry on until the end, except..."

"Except what?"

"Well ... I got this idea, Mam."

She closed her eyes momentarily. "Come on then. Let's have it."

"Not in here, Mam."

He took her downstairs and into the cafe.

"Why have we come in here?" she asked.

Joe thought it was the best place to tell her, so he made them both a hot drink and they sat in a booth.

While Joe explained his idea he braced himself for her to say no. She didn't look annoyed, though she didn't seem pleased either. "This would be for

Nonno," he said. "Not for us, or the cafe, but for Nonno. Then it'll be sold and over with. We'll go out with a bang."

Mam stared into the High Street. Joe followed her gaze, but all he saw were the raindrops scurrying down the window. "I know Nonno paid for Mimi to come over," she said. "That told me he wanted to give it one last try, so we will."

"The thing is, Mam," said Joe. "We'll need Mimi to help."

"I know."

"But she's just got a job in London."

"I'll see if she's willing to stay a little longer, to help with this," said Mam. "She's helped us already, I'm not blind to that. I objected to her being here at first. She's so confident – I don't just mean with cooking; it's like she's unstoppable. When I was her age I just bungled along – I was clueless, but she's amazing. She was right about the breakfasts and the coffee. I argued back only because I felt threatened. Silly, really. I even felt threatened by Mr Malewski – me, the granddaughter of an immigrant – when all he's doing is earning a living for his family, just like my granddad did."

She smiled at Joe. "You know when you cooked that pasta the other night..."

"*Puttanesca.*"

"Yeah... I was jealous."

"Jealous, of me?"

"Yes, in a way," said Mam. "I watched you cooking. You were concentrating so hard, I was worried for you."

"Wanted it to taste good."

"It did. I used to watch my mam cook, but I didn't have the confidence to ask her to show me how, not properly. Then when Mam died Nonno took over the cooking. He seemed to enjoy it, so I let him. I was embarrassed to try and cook anything in front of Mimi."

"But you *can* cook, Mam."

"Oh, yeah – fish fingers is about my limit."

"I love your fish fingers."

"Yeah."

"I do! It's my favourite meal."

Mam's lips went tight. "Thanks, love." She kissed him. "But I tell you what worries me..."

"What?"

"It's not how much this idea of yours will cost..." She stared him in the eye. "What worries me ... is that when this cafe is sold you'll feel resentful towards me."

"No, Mam," said Joe. "Nonno sees that the cafe's

finished. He doesn't blame you or anyone. If it's over, it's over. I see that now."

Mam held his hand. "We'll do this thing," she said. "It's a lovely idea."

"Thanks, Mam," said Joe. He was pleased. "Let's listen to some opera together."

"Oh, nothing depressing, mind."

Joe got up and went to the CD player. "I'll put on this Verdi chorus Nonno likes, from *Nabucco*. Lovely, it is. Oh, and I'm gonna write to Jamie, Mam."

"Jamie who?"

"Jamie Oliver."

"What for?"

"Advice, Mam."

"Right, fine," she said. "Whatever, Joe."

The *Va pensiero* chorus began.

"Oh, I know this," said Mam. "It's lovely, but don't tell me they're all about to die?"

"No, Mam – they're singing about home."

Joe held Mam's hand and they listened to the beautiful music.

FIFTY THREE

"I'm glad you can stay to help us, Mimi," said Joe as they walked along an alleyway.

"I want to," she said. "Is a great idea."

Joe stopped in front of a back doorway. "This is it."

"Are you sure this will work, Joe?"

"If he agrees, I'll do the rest."

They crept into the backyard. There were the remains of various heating boilers, as well as a few pipes strewn about. Joe could see a light on in an upstairs room. He picked up a stone and threw it at the window, then he hid behind two wheelie bins.

Nothing happened.

Joe tried again. This time the curtain parted and Combi opened the window, grinning like he'd won the lottery. "Mimi!"

"Hello, Combi," she said.

"Why didn't you come round the front?"

Mimi hesitated.

"It's private," Joe whispered.

"Is private," Mimi repeated. "About Joe."

"Oh," said Combi. "Not talking to him."

"I know," said Mimi. "He tell me what he say to you. Is very bad, Combi."

"Yeah. He's so uncool – uncool-*issimo*!"

Joe clenched his jaw.

"He's very, *very* sorry, Combi," said Mimi.

"So he should be," he said. "I mean, what my gramps did has nothing to do with me, does it?"

"No."

"Giving it large he was – well out of order."

"*Combi! Who you talking to?*" someone called from within.

"A beautiful girl in the backyard, Mam!" He grinned at Mimi.

Joe moaned.

"What was that?" Combi asked.

"A cat, I think," said Mimi.

"Sounded more like a dog," said Combi. "Did Joe tell you I can cook?"

Joe's mouth dropped open.

"No," said Mimi. "You cook?"

"Oh, aye, big-time cook, me," said Combi. "Always watching cookery programmes. See, I'm Welsh-Afro-Caribbean, so I like Cajun chicken, plantain ... and ... and Welsh cakes. You'll have to come round for dinner one evening. Just you though."

"I will," said Mimi. "If you forgive Joe."

"I'm not sure about that."

"Not even for me, Combi?"

"I will if I can have a free lunch in the cafe with you, Mimi – *just* you, and if Joe's *really* sorry."

"Oh, he is," said Mimi. "And yes, I cook you lunch, but I must go now."

Combi kissed his fingers and fluttered them at Mimi, and she blew him a kiss in return. Joe followed her out. He wanted to scream, but he waited until he was at a safe distance.

FIFTY FOUR

Joe, Combi and Bonner stood before the receptionist.

"Councillor Morgan is a very busy man," she said.

Joe thought she was being a bit snooty. "It's important."

"Important," repeated Bonner.

"Important-*issimo*," said Combi. "That's Italian for very important."

Joe pointed at him and nodded. "It is."

"He's in conference at the moment," she said.

"We can wait," said Joe. He turned and sat in a seat opposite the receptionist's desk. Combi and Bonner sat either side of him.

"What's her problem-o?" whispered Combi. "Like we're a bad smell."

Joe glanced at him. "Thanks for coming," he said. "You know ... after what happened..."

"Don't want to talk about it," said Combi. "I'm here and that's that."

"Well, I'm sorry," said Joe.

"So you should be."

"I am."

"Bad-*issimo*, you were."

"I thought you didn't wanna talk about it?" said Joe.

"Correct-*issmo*," said Combi.

Bonner turned to Joe. "Did Mimi tell you I'm only here cos she asked me?"

"She did."

"Future Mrs Bonner there, I tell you."

Joe shuddered at the idea.

Combi leaned close to him. "What did he say about Mimi?"

"He was asking after her."

"If he only knew," said Combi.

"Knew what?" asked Joe.

"About Mimi and me... Looking forward to my *free* lunch with her."

Joe nodded stiffly.

"Oh, and by the way," said Combi. "Next time you hide in my backyard try not to wear dayglo trainers."

"Right," said Joe. He wanted to change the subject so he said to the receptionist, "Cafe Merelli is serving lunches now."

"Really?" she said without looking up.

"Lovely food," said Bonner.

"Lovely," said Combi. "Better than the Chicken Box, even."

"Thanks," said Joe.

The receptionist huffed and picked up the phone. "They haven't gone," she whispered. "No... Three boys..." Then she put the phone down and said to them, "He'll see you now."

Councillor Rhys Morgan stood up as the boys entered his oak-panelled office.

"Always a pleasure to meet the youth of today," he said as he stretched a hand out to each boy. He was smiling until Bonner clasped his hand, making him wince.

"Now, what can I do for you young men?"

"The High Street is dying," said Joe.

"Dying," repeated Combi.

"Yes, it's a sad reflection of our times," the

councillor said as he glanced at his watch. "And, of course, our shopping habits are evolving – online retailers, online supermarkets..."

"Right," Joe said. "But people need a centre, otherwise there's no need for a town, is there? We might as well all live in pods and just open the door for deliveries only. No interaction, no community..."

Out of the corner of his eye Joe could see Combi pointing at him and nodding. The councillor looked perplexed. "The reason we came to see you," said Joe, "is to try and do something about it."

"Very good," Councillor Morgan said. "You'll go far."

"It's the anniversary of VE day soon."

"Yes!" he said.

"D'you know when it is?" asked Bonner.

"Of course," said the councillor.

Joe, Combi and Bonner waited. The councillor's fixed grin began to show signs of strain. "Remind me."

"May the eighth."

"That's it," he said. "Knew it was early May."

"I was thinking," said Joe. "We should do something to mark the occasion."

"I hear you," said Councillor Morgan. "A parade of cadets and Scouts – that sort of thing?"

Joe was disappointed. "No. Not at all."

Bonner shook his head. "Dull."

"Dull-*issimo*," said Combi.

"I was thinking more like a celebration," said Joe. "A food festival of the many cultures here in Bryn Mawr – to celebrate freedom and the end of oppression."

"Lovely idea," said the councillor. "In the school playground, yeah? I can arrange for a couple of bobbies to lend a hand."

Joe shook his head, followed by Combi and Bonner. "No. A food festival on the High Street, at night, with bunting, lights, fireworks and free food."

"Nice," said Bonner.

"Free food," said Combi. "Mmm."

"Free food?" asked the councillor. "Who would pay?"

"Well ... you – the Bryn Mawr Council," said Joe.

The councillor's eyes seemed to glaze over.

"Oh, and I think we'd need to stop the traffic," said Joe. "You can't have cars and buses going by when people are sampling delicacies from around the world."

"No," said Combi. "No cars."

"I like the idea of bunting and fireworks," said Bonner. Joe pointed at him and nodded.

"Fascinating," the councillor said. "You'll go far, Joe." He glanced at his watch again. "I'll take this into the Council Chamber for consideration ... but, of course, what with the cutbacks..." He stood up and led them out into the reception area. "Lovely meeting you boys, and... Yes, lovely indeed."

He left them standing and walked off down the corridor.

Joe felt glum – defeated at the first hurdle.

"He's a plank," said Combi.

"You should have made him an offer he couldn't refuse," said Bonner.

"Yeah. I should've," said Joe, and then he was struck by an idea.

"Councillor Morgan!" he called as he ran up to him.

The councillor turned. "I really must be going."

"But it's about your dad, Councillor Morgan," said Joe. "I found out something *really* interesting about your dad."

The councillor's eye twitched.

FIFTY FIVE

"What d'you mean, you don't want our usual chicken?" said Mr Patel.

"We want delicacies from your rich Indian culture."

Mr Patel shook his head. "Not interested."

"Hang on," said Combi. "What about all the money we've spent in the Chicken Box? Doesn't that count for anything?"

"Yes," said Mr Patel with a smirk. "Thanks for the business."

Bonner turned to the children waiting in line. "Right! Everybody out!"

The children turned and left the shop.

"Wait. Wait!" said Mr Patel in a panic. "What do I have to do?"

"Everyone back!" shouted Bonner.

The children filed back in.

"It must be cooked from fresh," said Joe to Mr Ling.

"Fresh? My food *is* fresh!"

Joe smiled. "Really?"

"Look, I'm not interested," said Mr Ling.

"Oh," said Joe. "Well, you won't mind if Mr Patel puts his food out in front, here."

"Patel?" said Mr Ling. "Why can't he have his food in front of *his* place?"

"It's too far up the street," said Combi.

"OK," said Mr Ling. "If Patel's doing it I'll do it."

"Give my food free?" said Mr Sadik. "Why?"

"Celebrating VE day," said Joe. "You don't want the Turkish community to get bad press, do you?"

Combi shook his head.

"Mr Malewski's going to lay out *three* tables. Three!" said Bonner.

"OK. If Malewski's doing it, I'll do it. Three tables... Huh!"

"Not just kebabs," said Joe. "Some baklava would be nice, to go with the coffee."

Mr Sadik frowned.

"This a joke?" said Mr Malewski.

"No," said Joe. "VE day – marking the end of World War Two in Europe. Didn't your dad fight in the war?"

"No. Too young."

"What about his dad?" asked Bonner.

"Free food! Crazy."

"Wait!" said Marta to her dad. "Listen."

"I'm disappointed, Mr Malewski," said Joe. "Have you forgotten the Polish night so soon?"

"This is business, Joe. You can't give food free."

"What if other people got to like Eastern European products?" said Joe. "Think about it. More interest. More sales."

"Yes!" said Marta. "Good business!"

"I got plenty customers."

Marta growled.

"If you don't get involved, Mr Malewski," said Joe. "You'll just draw attention to yourself in a bad way."

"What you mean 'bad way'?"

"Trading standards," said Combi. "They'll go, 'Why's Malewski not involved in this food festival?' and they'll think, 'Maybe he's got something to hide.' You get me?"

Combi, Joe and Bonner nodded in perfect synchronisation.

"We'll do it," said Marta.

FIFTY
SIX

Joe read the notes he'd made. "The meal is going to be in three courses."

"Yes, Joe," said Mam, sitting beside him and Mimi in the cafe.

"The first course is going to be tastes from around the world – Indian, Turkish, Chinese, Polish, Russian, and loads more – supplied by the takeaways and Mr Malewski. The second course will be Nonno's lasagne."

"Nonno's lasagne?"

"Yeah. Everyone likes lasagne," said Joe. "Got the recipe off him at the hospital, but we're going to do one with asparagus and one with minced beef *and* pork, which I found out is what proper Italians use." Mimi nodded. "Oh, and I want to cook it myself."

"You?" said Mimi.

"Yeah, with you two helping me, of course."

"Good on you, Joe," said Mam.

"So that means you and Mimi serving. Is that all right?"

Mimi and Mam glanced at each other. "Yes, Joe."

"And I think we should wear white shirts and black trousers."

"Uniforms?" said Mam.

"Dress code," said Joe. "It'll be smart. Professional, we'll be."

She rolled her eyes.

"Mam!"

"YES, Joe. Fine."

"Dessert will be sweet pizza and home-made *gelato*."

"Sweet pizza?" said Mimi. "What is it?"

"Combi gave me the idea – sort of. It's pizza with sweet toppings," said Joe. "We'll need to try it out – I found a recipe for a normal pizza base, but I'd add sugar and then toppings of sliced apple, banana and coconut."

"Sounds nice," said Mam.

Mimi pulled a face. "Why not have *tiramisu* or *panna cotta*?"

"Cos this'll be different," said Joe. "I'm going to dig out the old ice-cream machine for the *gelato* – Nonno says it's in the attic."

"If it still works," said Mam as she picked up Joe's guest list.

"Vaughan said he'd check it over for me," said Joe. "And, Mam, I'd like to get all the rips in the seating repaired. I got an estimate from a furniture repair man." He turned to his notes and pointed out the cost. "Please, Mam – be good to get it all done nice."

"OK," she said as she glanced down the guest list. "I can't believe Councillor Morgan's on here."

"It's amazing what you find out with a bit of digging around," said Joe.

"And he's coming?"

"Well ... I made him an offer he couldn't refuse."

"You what?"

"Lights and bunting are going up now, but he couldn't promise fireworks," said Joe. "Oh, and he said he's bringing someone from the *South Wales Echo*. Good publicity, Mam. I'll start on the list and phone round."

Joe got up, but then remembered something. "Oh,

and we need to clean the walls."

"The walls!"

"Yes, Mam. They *are* dirty. We can clean them ourselves, can't we?"

Mam glanced at Mimi.

"Yes, Joe," they said.

FIFTY SEVEN

"It looks like normal pizza," said Mam hovering in the doorway to the cafe.

"That's the idea," said Joe as he placed the sliced apples and banana in a regular pattern on the pizza base. He glanced at Mimi who still had the corners of her mouth pulled down. "But taste is more important than the look."

Finally, Joe sprinkled desiccated coconut over the top. "It looks like grated Parmesan!"

Mimi smiled and they placed the sweet pizza in the oven.

"Joe!" called Mam. "He's here!"

When Joe went into the cafe he saw a large car parked outside. He grinned. "It worked."

Councillor Morgan stepped out of the car and posed for the photographer. He entered the cafe with a reporter, who was taking notes.

"Fantastic," he said. "A classic Welsh-Italian cafe."

"Italian-Welsh, actually," said Joe.

Councillor Morgan turned to the reporter. "See, Joe came to me with this idea, and straight away I knew he was on to something."

"I'm from the *South Wales Echo*," said the reporter. "Can I ask you, Joe—"

He was interrupted by an announcement. "*Mr Dickens to Dr Foster, room three.*"

"What was that?" asked the councillor.

"Doctor's surgery announcements," said Mam.

"'Scuse me," said Mr Dickens, pushing past.

Joe began to explain his idea to the reporter when Mam shouted, "Bus for Ponty!"

A group of people got up to leave and Councillor Morgan was hustled out with them in the rush. Joe was still explaining to the reporter about what was happening that night as the councillor fought his way back into the cafe.

"What about that, Councillor?" asked the reporter.

"What about what?" he said, brushing himself down.

"Reimbursing the costs that Mr Merelli, and others, have incurred to offer free food this evening?"

"Mr who?"

"Mr Merelli," said the reporter, pointing at Joe. "Joe Merelli."

Joe smiled. "It's Joe Davis, actually, née Merelli."

"Ah, well..." said Councillor Morgan. "Naturally, the Bryn Mawr Council wants to do everything it can to support local initiatives..."

"Is that a 'yes'?"

"No."

"I got this voucher scheme an' all," said Joe.

"Voucher scheme?" asked the reporter.

"People with free time, including the unemployed," said Joe, "would earn a voucher by working in the community. Then they could cash in the voucher for a free meal, see."

"Sounds terrific," said Gwen. "I'm a pensioner and I'd love someone to tidy my garden."

"I'll do it for a couple of vouchers," said Vaughan.

There were murmurs from the other customers.

"What about that?" the reporter asked the councillor. "Sounds good to me."

Councillor Morgan's eye twitched. "I'd have to take this—"

"To the Council Chamber, I know," said Joe. "And

I got this other idea for free cookery lessons."

"Free cookery lessons?"

"Yeah," said Joe. "We can improve the eating habits of people in Bryn Mawr."

"Healthy food," said Mimi.

"Like this," said Vaughan as he lifted his plate under the councillor's nose. "Oh, you should try it. *Cannelloni con spinaci e funghi* – that's spinach and mushrooms to you. *Buonissimo.*"

"I second that," said Gwen. "*Molto buonissimo.*"

"Something smells nice," said the reporter. "Apple pie, is it?"

"No. Sweet pizza," said Joe as he speed-dialled the cafe phone from his mobile. The phone rang and he gave Mam a nudge.

"Hello," said Mam down the phone. "Oh, just a moment... Joe, it's Jamie."

"Jamie? Jamie who?" he asked.

"Jamie Oliver."

"Tell him I'm busy, Mam," said Joe. "Busy with Councillor Morgan."

"Is that *the* Jamie Oliver?" the reporter asked.

"Yeah, but he can call back," said Joe. "Now, about tonight..."

FIFTY EIGHT

The bus driver thought Joe was mad to ask, but after a phone call to Councillor Morgan it was arranged for the buses to block the High Street after seven o'clock, and divert cars around the backstreets. Mr Malewski, Dariusz and Marta began to set out some tables with products from Eastern Europe, and Mr Ling, Mr Sadik and Mr Patel did the same with tasters from their takeaways. The shops that were closed kept their window lights on to brighten the street.

Mam and Mimi were helping Joe prepare the food for the evening, and Vaughan checked the old ice-cream maker. "Seems A-OK," he said.

"Thanks," said Joe as he brushed the four sweet pizzas he'd made with a honey glaze. He stood back to look at them as if he'd just finished a painting.

"They're lovely," said Mam.

"Hope they taste as good as the trial one we did. They'll need to go in the oven when we start serving the main course. Now we can start on the lasagne."

Joe poured the meat into the frying pan with the onions and garlic, and added the spices.

"And remember, Mam," he said. "Nonno needs to be here by—"

"I know, I know," she said.

There was a roll of distant thunder. "Aw, no!" said Joe, putting his hands to his face. "No rain. Not tonight, please."

"Get on the phone to Councillor Morgan," said Mam. "Perhaps he can sort something."

Mimi laughed.

"Funny," said Joe. "Oh, Vaughan. Have you put up the speakers?"

"Soon as I finish here, Joe," he replied.

"What are the speakers for?" Mam asked.

"The music."

"Music?"

Joe left Mam perplexed and went to have a look in the cafe.

All the ugly taped-up repairs had been replaced by neat red stitching. Each of the tables had tablecloths and candles, and a fixed menu with veggie options.

Joe felt a sudden wave of panic. "What if they don't come, Mam?" he said.

"It's a free dinner," she said. "People round y'ere aren't going to miss out on that."

"Joe!" shouted Mimi. "Don't leave the food!"

He ran back. "Sorry!"

The lasagne sauce was thick and ruddy, and it smelled beautiful. The ice-cream maker made a low grinding noise as it churned on the table. Two large lasagne baking trays were cleaned.

"These haven't seen the light of day for thirty years, I reckon," said Mam.

They began to prepare the two lasagne – one for the meat and one for the asparagus. They continued layering until the two baking trays were full. Joe grated Parmesan cheese over each one and they put them in the oven.

"Phew," said Mam.

"Thanks, Mam. Thanks, Mimi," said Joe. "I appreciate it and I hope the guests do too."

Mam kissed him just as there was a knock at

the cafe door.

"Joe!" said Mimi. "They're here – the first guests."

Gwen entered, dressed up to the nines, as was Vaughan and his mother. Mam went round the tables and started lighting the candles.

"Oh, beautiful," said Gwen.

Joe watched from the kitchen as more and more of the guests arrived, taking their seats at the tables. Councillor Morgan sat in the corner with his wife, looking distinctly uptight. Combi and his parents shared a booth with Bonner and his mother, who barely reached up to his shoulder. No one was talking, and Joe sensed they were a little uncomfortable.

Mam came into the kitchen. "Joe," she said. "That's it – all the guests are here."

Joe stepped into the cafe. "Thank you for coming," he said to them. "This a free meal, including the wine. It's a celebration, and I hope you enjoy the food."

"Are you going to tell us why you invited us now?" asked Gwen.

"Soon," said Joe. "Let's eat first." He dialled a number on his mobile. "We're ready."

A short while later Mr Malewski, Marta, Dariusz, Mr Ling, Mr Patel and Mr Sadik began to bring through the starters and offer them to the guests.

FIFTY NINE

Joe popped his head through the door now and again, to see how things were going in the cafe. He was pleased to see that Mr Malewski, Marta and the others had entered into the spirit of the occasion and were describing the tasters they were offering from their different countries.

By the time the main course was ready people were chatting merrily.

The two types of lasagne were cut into neat squares and plated with a generous sprinkling of Parmesan cheese. Joe watched anxiously as the guests tucked in.

The *oohs* and *aahs* he heard were like food to an empty stomach, but it was the sight of the cafe full of diners chatting in the glow of candlelight that touched him more.

"Mam," he said. "Come with me."

"Still serving, Joe."

"Mimi can manage. It'll only take a few minutes."

He took Mam's hand and went out into the alley.

"Where are we going?"

"Wait and see."

They reached the High Street and Joe led Mam across the road. He turned her to face the cafe, which sparkled with light. "Look. You got to admit, Mam, it's beautiful."

She pulled Joe to her and kissed the top of his head.

"It is, Joe. I've never seen it till now. It *is* beautiful."

They stood watching Mimi moving from table to table and the customers eating contentedly. Then Joe saw the ambulance approaching. The timing was perfect.

Mam and Joe greeted Nonno as he was helped out of the ambulance, followed by Dad. When they entered the cafe the customers stood up and began to applaud.

"Welcome home, Papà," said Mam.

SIXTY

Joe watched from the kitchen doorway as the sweet pizza slices were served, each with a dollop of homemade ice cream.

"Pizza for afters?" said Combi.

"It's sweet pizza," said Mam.

Combi's eyes lit up. He was the first to cut into the pizza slice and try it. His eyes rolled back. "Oh, lovely. Hot apple and banana."

Joe smiled and felt proud as he watched people enjoying his new dessert.

"Bravo, Joe," said Mimi. "Very clever."

Nonno took a seat behind the counter as Joe

stepped out of the kitchen to a round of applause.

"I promised we'd say why you were all invited here tonight," said Joe. "Well, the main reason was to celebrate the return of Nonno, or Beppe to you. The other reason was to thank you all."

He took out the list.

"During the war in nineteen forty, Nonno was making deliveries for Mr Lewis, the butcher – that was your dad," Joe said to Mr Lewis. "I know it was a long time ago, but you're here because your dad gave Nonno a job when others would have nothing to do with him."

"I was a toddler," said Mr Lewis, "but I remember."

Nonno raised a glass to him.

"Gwen," said Joe.

"Ooh, what?"

"On one of Nonno's deliveries he was set upon by some boys, and your mam saved him. She told them off and sent them on their way."

"Good on her!" said Gwen.

"Mrs Bonner and Tony," said Joe.

Bonner blushed as he looked around.

"Your dad and granddad was a policeman – PC Williams."

"He was," said Bonner's mam.

"Did you know he tipped off Nonno that the army

were coming to arrest his dad?"

"No, I didn't."

"Well, he did, and it gave him enough time to get away. If your granddad had been found out he would have lost his job. It was a great thing to do. Thank you."

Mrs Bonner began to cry. "There there, Mam," said Bonner with a firm pat on her shoulder, making her wince.

"Vaughan!" said Joe.

Vaughan stood up, and his mam pulled him back down into his seat.

"Your granddad, Dai Gwynn, was a miner," said Joe.

"I know."

Joe pointed at the photograph of Vito Merelli. "Dai smuggled my great-granddad, disguised as a miner, back into Bryn Mawr and into this cafe."

"Did he really?"

"But not only that, he hid Vito in his house when the army wanted to arrest him for being an enemy alien. Dai Gwynn could have been arrested himself if he was found out."

Nonno raised his hand to Vaughan and his mam and they sat up with pride.

"And that's where the rest of you come in," said

Joe to the other guests. "I'll let Nonno tell you what happened."

He turned to the tape recorder and pressed play.

"Slowly, over the following weeks and months, people in Bryn Mawr took turns to shelter Papà in their homes. It was a secret, held only by those who could be trusted. They realised he was no threat and to keep him away from his family was inhuman. Every few days he went to a different house. Each family gave him food and somewhere to sleep, and as it turned out they sheltered him over the next four years. He was never caught, but one day he sent me a message – it simply said, 'Dai loro da mangiare,' which meant 'feed them'. It was the one way he could thank them..."

Joe stopped the tape and turned to the customers. "My great-granddad went to different homes to avoid capture – different families in Bryn Mawr: the Evanses, the Morrises – that was your great-granddad, Combi, on your father's side..."

Combi grinned.

"...The Thomases, the Matthewses, the Zecchinis, the Cohens, the Llewellyns, the Morgans..." Joe nodded at Councillor Morgan, who dabbed a tear from his eye. "...And the Davises," said Joe. "That's right, Dad, even your grandparents. You all took turns on a rota. You saved him from deportation right up to VE day in nineteen forty-five. That's why you're all here. We wanted to thank you with this meal."

There was silence, then Joe, Nonno, Mam and Mimi began to applaud the guests. Joe quickly dialled a phone number. "Now would be good," he said into the phone.

He switched on the radio and adjusted the dial to get a good reception for the station.

"And now, for an extra event to mark VE day in Bryn Mawr," the DJ announced, *"here is Beppe Merelli with his own recollections of that day..."*

There was silence for a moment and then Nonno's voice.

"On May the eighth everyone came to the town centre. The war was over. You could feel the joy and relief in the air. It was beautiful. But the moment I'll never forget was when Papà stepped back into the cafe. He just walked in, just like that, as if he'd only been away for a few hours. He was a free man, out in the open for all to see. He went upstairs, washed and dressed, then he came down into the cafe in his white coat and hat for the first time in over four years. People

welcomed him back with open arms, and he showed no ill will.

That night a lovely thing happened. People wandered about in the centre of Bryn Mawr, like they were having a passeggiata. Papà put a record on his old gramophone. It was the Va pensiero chorus from Verdi's Nabucco. He started singing along and everyone joined in, because the Welsh know it – it's the song about everyone's homeland. The words are beautiful: 'Fly my thoughts on golden wings. Go to the slopes and hills, where soft, sweet breezes take us to our native land...'

It was a special thing to see and hear. The shop lights seemed to shine that bit more brightly. Papà made food. He cooked and cooked, as if he was making up for all the lost hours. The last of his preserves were used up. He fed everyone – he shared it all."

They listened in silence until the DJ said, "*Now, if you make your way to the Bryn Mawr High Street there's a free food festival. Yes, that's right, free food from different countries, and all provided by Bryn Mawr shopkeepers to celebrate VE day – Victory in Europe. Here's the chorus from Verdi's Nabucco, as was just mentioned. We're glad you're back, Mr Merelli...*"

The music started, but it wasn't just playing in the cafe, it was playing through speakers and into the street. The glorious chorus filled the night air.

Joe nodded at Councillor Morgan, who said into his phone, "OK. Now."

The lines of decorative fairy lights snapped on – Bryn Mawr High Street was ablaze with light, and it wasn't long before people were milling around and tasting the food. "Look, Nonno," said Joe. "They're taking a *passeggiata*."

Nonno's eyes glistened with tears.

He tapped his chest and blew Joe a kiss.

SIXTY ONE

It was late that night when Joe was sitting in the cafe with Nonno, Mam, Mimi and Dad, finishing off the last of the wine. It had started to rain, but the lights of the High Street still shone brightly.

"I'll never forget tonight, Joe," said Mam. "Proud of you, I am."

"And you, Mam, and you, Mimi," he said.

"You *all* did it together," said Nonno. "Proud of you all."

They clinked glasses.

"Oh, by the way, Joe," said Mam. "Natalie was asking me something about tonight – her dad was

Johnny Corbett, right?"

"That's right."

"And you invited them cos you found out that Combi's great-granddad on his father's side was one of the families that had taken in Nonno's dad during the war?"

Joe stared up at the ceiling. "Yeah."

"But how could that be?" said Mam. "I know your great-granddad was moved around town to all the different families, but I'm pretty sure that didn't include a family who were living in *Jamaica* at the time."

"Oh, Joe," said Nonno.

"Well, I felt bad about what I did to Combi and I wanted him included."

"But what about the others, Joe?" said Mam. "Please tell me they were *all* really—"

"Oh, yeah, *they* were all legit – promise," said Joe. "All legitimate relatives of those who helped us, apart from Combi."

"Oh, good."

"And Councillor Morgan," Joe added.

"Councillor Morgan!" said Mam. "So his folks never helped us during the war?"

"No. His family were from North Wales."

"So why did you include him?"

"Well, I figured if I invited him he couldn't refuse, see."

Mam rolled her eyes. "'An offer he couldn't refuse'."

"Right. So if he was involved, he'd be useful – stopping the traffic. The lights. The reporter... He was *very* useful."

Joe's eyebrow arched up.

Mimi, Mam and Dad stared at him, and then Nonno started making a funny noise. Mam panicked and went to phone for an ambulance.

"It's OK," said Dad. "I think he's laughing."

Nonno started banging the table. He had tears in his eyes and was laughing uncontrollably.

Mam turned to Joe. "You're mad."

She held her fingers together and shook her hand.

"Mam!" said Joe. "You've gone all Italian!"

She kissed him and held his face in her hands. "Joe. You are ... *bellissimo*."

SIXTY TWO

Mimi waited for the train with Joe, Mam, Vaughan, Marta, Bonner and Combi. No one spoke. As the train pulled in, Joe's throat was so tight he felt as if he'd never be able to swallow again.

"Thanks for all you've done, Mimi," said Mam as they hugged.

Mimi turned to Vaughan and kissed him on each cheek. He gave her a cauliflower and said, "Promise you'll come back to visit us."

"I promise."

Marta held up a small bag for Mimi. "Polish goodies," she said. "We have lots of new Welsh customers now, because of last night. Good business!"

"Bye, Mimi," said Combi. "I bought you some Wagon Wheels for the journey."

She kissed him and then turned to Bonner.

"The Mawr won't be the same without you, Mimi," he said.

"Oh, so sweet," she replied, kissing him on the cheek.

"No one's ever called me 'sweet'," said Bonner. "Apart from my mam."

Lastly, Mimi turned to Joe.

"I hope one day you find Giovanni," he said. "Or *a* Giovanni."

"Beautiful Joe," she said as she kissed him.

Joe was sure he could hear the love duet from *La Bohème* as he managed to say, "*Ciao*, Mimi."

The stationmaster blew his whistle and Mimi stepped up into the train doorway.

She wiped away her tears and blew them a kiss. "*Ciao*."

They waved. "*Ciao*, Mimi."

The train pulled out.

Joe decided he hated trains, because once they started going there was nothing you could do to stop them.

They all made their way back to Bryn Mawr in

silence, and by the time they reached the High Street it had started to rain.

Mam stopped. "Joe," she said, staring at the cafe.

"Yes, Mam."

"Were you serious about wanting to take over the cafe when you leave school?"

"But you're selling it."

"Just answer the question."

"Yes."

"You won't mind standing behind that counter eight hours a day?"

"No."

"Looking at miserable faces and an empty High Street?"

"They're not always miserable and the High Street is not always empty."

Mam offered him her hand. "Congratulations," she said. "You're the proud new owner of Cafe Merelli."

As Joe took her hand he was still thinking of the train door closing on Mimi, but when Mam's offer dawned on him he burst into tears.

"What's the matter?"

He fell into her arms. "Can't help it, Mam – I'm Italian."

"Oh, my God," said Mam. "I just realised, Joe."

"What?"

"We gotta cook lunch ... without Mimi!"

"Panick-*issimo*!"

Joe and Mam rushed into the cafe kitchen, and pulled out pans and ingredients. They continually bumped into each other as they prepared the food. They cried as they chopped onions. They broke plates. They burned food – not to mention their fingers – and they even forgot to put the oven on.

"Everything OK?" Dad asked from the doorway of the cafe.

"NO!" snapped Joe and Mam at the same time.

"I got four orders for the pasta and two for soup," said Dad.

Joe looked at Mam and saw the fear in her face.

There was a knock at the back door. "I'll get it," said Dad as he walked past them.

He opened the door.

Mimi was standing there in the rain. "I don't want to go to London," she said.

"Oh," said Mam.

Mimi sniffed the air. "Something burning?"

Mam turned to Joe. "Something burning, Joe."

"Yes," he said. "It is."

"You want me to help?" asked Mimi.

"Well ... you can give us a hand," said Mam. "And while you're with us I'll split the lunch profits with you, fifty–fifty, and ... and you can teach me to cook..."

"Yes," said Joe. "I want to learn too."

Mimi dropped her bag. "OK. Let's begin."

SIXTY THREE

Lunch was in full swing and the cafe was packed out.

Joe was happier than he'd ever been in his life. Doctors' announcements came regularly and bus passengers were in and out. Sometimes they decided to catch the next one so that they could stay and have the special dish of the day.

Mam stirred the contents of a large saucepan on the hob.

Nonno sat nearby and watched with Joe.

"See how thick it is?" said Mimi.

"I see."

"Is reduced," she said. "So the flavour is strong. Try."

Mam tasted it. "Mmm. Joe, try it."

"Lovely," said Joe.

Vaughan came into the kitchen. "Your dad says he's ready!"

"Oh, right."

Nonno placed his old straw hat on Joe's head, and Mam straightened his tie. "You look great," she said.

"Thanks." He walked into the busy cafe. "Hello, Gwen."

She smiled. "Hello Joe. Oh, smart, you are."

"Yes indeed," said Vaughan, who was serving behind the counter.

"Everything OK for you?" Joe asked.

"Dandy," said Vaughan. "Serving customers, chatting, free lunches and a minimum wage. What's not to love – *contentissimo*, I am."

Joe stopped to look at the photographs of his great-granddad outside the cafe in nineteen twenty-nine, and Nonno in nineteen fifty-three, then he went outside.

He positioned himself in front of the cafe with his arms folded. Dad looked through the camera. "You're a bit serious."

Joe smiled.

"That's better. OK, hold it."

Then Joe had an idea. "Wait, Dad!"

He went back into the cafe and behind the counter where Mam was standing.

"What have you forgotten?" she asked.

Joe took her hand. "You, Mam."

"No, Joe. Look at the state of me."

"You're fine." He led her outside and they stood in front of Cafe Merelli, together. Dad took the picture.

It was framed and hung on the cafe wall the very next day – the third and fourth generations of the Cafe Merelli management.

SIXTY FOUR

Joe and Combi were out of breath as they walked up the hill. The whole of Bryn Mawr lay below them. "This looks a good spot," said Joe.

"Why so far?" asked Combi.

"D'you wanna be seen?"

Joe started undressing.

"What are you doing?" asked Combi.

"Getting my kit on. What about yours?"

"What's wrong with what I'm wearing?"

"Combi, when was the last time you saw Usain Bolt running in a parka and a rucksack?" Combi shrugged and reluctantly took off his bag and coat.

They stood side by side. "We'll head towards that road sign," said Joe.

"OK. Marks. Set—"

"No! It's not a race, Combi! We're jogging, all right? Limber up first."

Joe tried to touch his toes but only got as far as his knees.

Combi watched.

"You need to stretch, Combi," said Joe. "Otherwise you'll strain yourself."

"Look. Do whatever you've got to do but stop giving me orders."

"Right. Road sign. Ready? Go."

They ran, but after only a few strides both boys were leaning on each other and gasping for breath. They lay down on the road, side by side.

"I think I'm dying," said Combi.

"Cos we ran," said Joe. "Jogging, it was meant to be."

Combi crawled to his rucksack. He pulled out a bottle of Coke.

"Oh, Combi!" said Joe.

"I've earned it – knackered-*issimo*!"

Joe got to his feet and gazed down on to Bryn Mawr. He could see the High Street and Cafe Merelli. "Mam said I could paint my cafe."

Combi stood beside him. "What colour?"

"Blue, I was thinking."

"Green would be better – warmer."

Joe thought about it. "Green's not out of the question."

He heard a noise and turned round to see two girls coming down the hill fast, on bicycles. They were screaming. Joe stared at one of the girls – she was big and angry-looking. When their eyes met Joe heard a rumble of thunder. *"Pattacrack!"* he said.

Combi looked at him. "What d'you say?"

"I said, who are they?" asked Joe.

"Gemma Matthews and her weird mate, Cowgirl."

"She doesn't look weird," said Joe as they put their coats back on.

"You know what would go down a treat now?" said Combi.

"No. Not the Chicken Box," said Joe.

"Yeah," said Combi. "Go on."

"No," said Joe. "But I could knock up some sweet pizza."

Combi swallowed. "Nice. With chocolate spread this time?"

"No," said Joe. "Too sweet. But I could make one with pears, or strawberries. And I tell you what – we could cut it into triangles and sell it. Take on the

Chicken Box – a healthy snack alternative."

"Mr Patel wouldn't like that."

"Free market," said Joe. "Business is business."

"Can you make some now?"

"Only if you don't get any chicken and chips."

"Deal."

Joe put his arm round Combi's shoulder.

"What's with the arm?"

"I'm Italian, Combi. And you're my mate – my best mate."

"Fair enough," said Combi slipping his arm over Joe's shoulder.

It began to rain as they made their way back down towards Bryn Mawr.

Joe looked up at the grey clouds and smiled.

"*Bellissimo*," he said.

ACKNOWLEDGEMENTS

I'm very grateful to Kate Wilson and the team at Nosy Crow for publishing my second book, with a special mention to Dom Kingston, head of publicity, for his super-efficient organisation and support of my *Cowgirl* school, library and bookshop events all over the country.

It was a great pleasure to work once again with my editor, Kirsty Stansfield – always so enthusiastic, patient and kind. Thanks, Kirsty, and latterly to Fiona Scoble.

I greatly appreciate the continued support and advice of my agent, Claire Wilson, together with Lexie Hamblin.

A special thanks to Paulette Pelosi and David Evans who have been extremely helpful in my research of Italians in Wales and the *Arandora Star* tragedy (www.arandorastarwales.us). I'm also grateful to the late Colin Hughes for his wonderful book, *Lemon, Lime and Sarsaparilla* (Seren Books), about the Italian community in Wales.

Thanks to Bethan Hughes for checking over the glimpse of Welsh in *Sweet Pizza*.

I'm grateful to my sister Barbara and my partner Isabelle for helping me with the recipes.

And a special mention to all the librarians for organising events and welcoming me so warmly in Abergavenny, Bedfordshire, Barnet, Barry, Cambridgeshire, Cardiff, Carmarthen, Cheltenham, Denbighshire, Gloucester, Haringey, Medway, Merthyr Tydfil, Oswestry, Penarth, Southend, Stroud, Suffolk, Swansea and Westminster. I'll be happy to come back with *Sweet Pizza*!

G.R. Gemin

HISTORICAL NOTE

Vito Merelli is a fictional character, but his experience of the sinking of the *SS Arandora Star* is based on a real event that cost the lives of over 800 men.

At the end of June 1940 the *SS Arandora Star* sailed from Liverpool with interned Italians and Germans aboard. Its destination was Canada. Early in the morning of 2nd July it was hit by a torpedo from a German U-boat.

Figures vary but among those who died were 58 crew members, 175 Germans and 486 Italians. Fifty-three of the Italians were from Wales.

Many survivors of the sinking were brought back to the UK and put on board another ship, the *HMT Dunera*, which sailed to Australia just eight days after the *Arandora Star* sank. The *Dunera* was also attacked by a submarine, but it continued its voyage and reached Australia.

Memorials to the *Arandora Star* victims can be viewed in St David's Cathedral in Cardiff, St Peter's Italian Church in London, St Michael's Church in Birmingham, the Italian Cloister Garden at St Andrew's Cathedral in Glasgow and at Pier Head in Liverpool.

In Italy there are memorials at Barga, Bratto and a chapel for the victims in the cemetery at Bardi.

The *Arandora Star* website contains information, first-hand recollections and many stories: www.arandorastarwales.us.

AUTHOR'S NOTE ON OPERA

Opera is weird, but at the same time I think it's brilliant. I say it's weird because if you've never heard or seen it before, it's basically people standing on stage and screaming. You may have seen a stage musical, like *Cats* or *Oliver*, but opera singers don't need microphones because they train their voices to sing more loudly than normal. It's amazing to hear, but it is a sort of controlled screaming – like I say, it's weird.

If you can get over the fact that it's not realistic at all, then I promise you opera is brilliant. I started listening to opera when I was only nine or ten, mainly because my dad was listening to it all the time. You can get totally absorbed in the drama. In fact, if you think about it, a good film or an animation is not real, but that doesn't stop you watching and becoming completely drawn-in by the story.

In the eighteenth and nineteenth centuries there

was no such thing as cinema, so people went to the theatre and the opera for entertainment. Composers like Mozart, Rossini, Verdi and Puccini composed operas based on books and plays that were popular at the time – just like today when they make films and plays based on popular books like *Harry Potter*. The storyline of some operas are ridiculous, but you need to bear in mind that they were written at a time when people liked melodramatic stories (that means stories that are a bit over-the-top). Mind you, I think most soap operas today are pretty over-the-top too.

Operas are nearly always about love, but a lot are also about death and murder too, so you need to be careful which one you listen to – I wouldn't want you to be bored with the first one you try.

If you think you'd like comic opera, that's light and easy to listen to, then you could try Mozart's *The Marriage of Figaro* (*Le Nozze di Figaro*) or Rossini's *The Barber of Seville* (*Il Barbiere di Siviglia*). They are both full of fun, and jam-packed with lovely music.

Giuseppe Verdi is my favourite opera composer. He wanted to thrill and entertain people. You could say he was a bit like the Steven Spielberg of his day – Verdi wanted to compose operas that were fast-paced, dramatic and full of great music. So if you think you like the sound of his operas, then I suggest Verdi's *Macbeth*, *Rigoletto*, *La Traviata*, *Aida* or *Otello*.

Puccini's operas are great too – full of gorgeous music that's moving and beautiful. You could try *La Bohème* or *Madama Butterfly* (I warn you – they are both very sad), or *Turandot*, which is like a fairy-tale opera.

Most operas are sung in Italian, so you'll have to read the story before, or follow with a libretto that tells you what the characters are saying. You can also find opera recordings in English, although, to be honest, you still might not understand what they are saying. At your local library you might be able to borrow opera CDs and DVDs, or you could even find out if there are operas being performed live near you.

You can find more information at Welsh National Opera (www.wno.org.uk), English National Opera (www.eno.org), Northern Ireland Opera (www. niopera.com), Scottish Opera (www.scottishopera. org.uk), Opera North (www.operanorth.co.uk) and The Royal Opera (www.roh.org.uk).

I hope you'll give it a try.

RECIPES

Cooking can be great fun and very satisfying. It's also a lot cheaper and healthier than buying ready-meals. As Mimi says, "a pasta sauce is easy", and you can use it to make lots of different types of sauce for pasta.

A basic tomato sauce (for four people)

INGREDIENTS
A tin of chopped plum tomatoes (or you can use a tin of whole plum tomatoes and mash them with a potato masher)
Tomato purée (you get it in a tube or a small tin)
Two tablespoons of olive oil, or a knob of butter.
Half an onion
A clove of garlic
Basil – fresh or dried.
Salt and pepper.

METHOD
Dice the onion and the garlic then fry them in the olive oil or butter.

Once the onion has softened, turn the hob down to a low heat and add the tin of chopped tomatoes. Add the basil, salt and pepper to taste. I like to add a tablespoon of tomato puree to give a little more flavour and colour as well.

Stir it and then let it simmer for about 20 to 25 minutes, until the sauce has thickened. Taste the sauce as you cook it, to see if it needs more seasoning.

That's the basic sauce, but if you want to make it a more interesting meal you could add things. For example, to keep it vegetarian, you could add a mug of frozen peas (add them after you've been cooking the tomatoes for about ten minutes). Frozen peas will thaw straight away, and you'll end up with a nice tomato and pea pasta sauce.

To cook the pasta you need about 80 grams of pasta per person (it can be any pasta shape you like, such as spaghetti or fusilli or rigatoni). Remember to follow the instructions on the packet, because some pasta can be cooked in five minutes but others need ten or fifteen minutes in boiling water. The pasta is ready when it's not too soft and not too hard, like Mimi says, "al dente". Drain it and return it to the pot you cooked it in, so then you can mix the sauce in with the pasta. Serve it in bowls or plates and sprinkle grated Parmesan cheese over it. Then you can eat sitting around a table and practice your Italian gestures!

Here are some other suggestions:

Tuna pasta is lovely and simple – just follow the instructions for the basic sauce above, then when it's done take the pan off the heat and mix in a tin of tuna (make sure you drain the oil or water from the tin of tuna before you mix it in).

Amatriciana is a great pasta dish if you like bacon. You'll need to slice up about three rashers of bacon, or use Pancetta, which is little cubes of bacon in a sachet that you can get in most supermarkets. Follow the instructions for the basic tomato sauce above (you could even include the peas), but fry the bacon or Pancetta with the onion and garlic at the beginning. You also need to add some chilli, dried or fresh, depending how hot you want it – I usually add half a teaspoon of dried chilli powder. (Be careful you don't accidently rub some chilli in your eyes after you've touched it as it stings!)

Pasta Bolognese uses minced beef. Fry half an onion and garlic with about 500g of minced beef. Fry it for about ten minutes, until the beef is browned, and then follow the instructions for the basic sauce above, but this sauce needs longer cooking time – about 35 to 40 minutes.

SWEET PIZZA RECIPE

The Italians don't really make sweet pizza. It exists, but it's an adaptation of normal pizza. You can find recipes online, but I think, in general, they are far too sweet. So here's a simple recipe for sweet pizza with sliced apples and bananas.

INGREDIENTS

250g of plain flour
Salt
Caster sugar
Olive oil
Baking powder
Milk
2 apples
1 ripe banana

METHOD

Before you start to make the pizza, heat the oven to 200°C or Gas mark 6.

For the pizza base, seive 250g of plain flour into a large bowl, then add a teaspoon of salt, 2 tablespoons of sugar and 1 teaspoon of baking powder. Mix these together.

Make a hole in the middle of the mixture and put in 3 tablespoons of oil. Mix it with your hands until it becomes like breadcrumbs. Then, little by little, add 4 tablespoons of milk and about a quarter of a mug of water, mixing them in as you go, to make a dough. It should become soft and not too sticky. Be careful – it can get messy.

Drizzle one tablespoon of olive oil onto a square oven tray, or pizza tray, and sprinkle with a little flour – this prevents the pizza base sticking to the tray. Roll the dough as thin as possible (about three or four millimetres unless you prefer a thicker base) and lay it on the oven tray. You may have to stretch it gently with your fingers to cover the area. It can be made into a circle or a square.

Peel and core the 2 apples, and slice them finely. Peel the ripe banana and slice it finely too. Leaving a 1½ centimetre border around the edge of the dough, arrange the sliced apples and banana in a single layer so that it looks like a pizza. Brush the border with a little milk and sprinkle the pizza with 3 tablespoons of sugar, or drizzle over a little honey. You can also sprinkle it with desiccated coconut or cinnamon. Finally, brush it with olive oil.

Cook in the oven for about 15 minutes – it doesn't take long. Cut it into triangular slices and eat it hot or cold. You can also invent your own toppings … sliced pear, or grapes, or strawberries, or you could add ground almonds. I'm sure you could come up with some nice ideas.

There are lots and lots of great recipes to try online – the BBC Food website (ww.bbc.co.uk/food) is very good and has lots of recipes from many different cultures.

Best wishes, or, as Joe would say, *Tanti auguri!*

Giancarlo